The Secret

(annotated)

By G. H. Teed

Illustrated by H. Radcliffe Wilson.

First published in the Union Jack magazine,
New series, No. 1482; 12 March 1932.

Stillwoods Edition

Stillwoods.Blogspot.Ca

Catalogue Information:
Title: The Secret (annotated)
Author: G. H. Teed
Edited by Doug Frizzle
Illustrated by: H. Radcliffe Wilson.
First published in the Union Jack magazine, New series, No. 1482; 12 March 1932.
This Edition by: Stillwoods, 2024
ISBN Canada: 978-1-998819-38-6
Blog: Stillwoods.Blogspot.Ca
Author Blog: http://ghteed.blogspot.com/
Storefront: http://www.lulu.com/spotlight/lulubook22

Keywords: Sexton Blake, Tinker, England.

https://tinyurl.com/ve25d42s This link should go to a spreadsheet of all known Teed stories. The list is annotated with various information on the stories and my progress with recapturing the work. The library of Teed's stories increases almost weekly. Check at Lulu.Com for the publications. Search for (space)Teed. /drf

Cautionary Note: This series of books by Stillwoods is intended to make the stories of G. H. Teed, born in New Brunswick, Canada, available to collectors and researchers. The editor, or rather digitizer has not altered the original publication.

This story may contain language and racial terms that are not appropriate today. I apologize for them; I know that the author was using his voice to excite and entertain an adventurous English audience. These works were published from 82 to 110 years ago. Most every work has characters of redeeming ethnicity within.

I hope you enjoy and share these stories; I have.

Doug Frizzle

Introduction to the Annotated Edition

- Facsimile Reproduction
- Supplementary Information
- Historical Context
- Collectors' Commentary
- Author Biographical Notes

This is my first 'Annotated Stillwoods Edition' of a Teed story. It is making its appearance 92 years after the original publication.

In fact though most of the previous works have included all of the bullets listed above. Publishers new rules require public domain works such as this to be special —and appended with a specifier in the title.

This Stillwoods collection is about the author G. H. Teed. The great majority of his 500+ stories were written anonymously. They also, at the time, were issued under copyright —under the Sexton Blake banner. Teed wrote from 1913 until his death at the end of 1938. Since these works were anonymous, no-one knew he was a Canadian —or at least I have never seen a mention.

Teed's novels appeared in 'pulps' mostly —magazines with cheap paper, and issued mostly on a weekly basis. In original format, they are difficult to obtain today in undamaged condition. And they can be expensive!

Now relating to 'Sexton Blake'. My opinion is that at any time there was a core stable of maybe six authors producing these stories. The editor chose the stories, and the sequence of publication.

There was a 'formula'; we have the detective and his assistant. We have a locale somewhere in the world. There is often some relationship of the story with world events of the day. And also, a key was that the villains were recurring, so they were defeated but escaped, so that they could appear in a subsequent issue!

Now regarding this issue, 'The Secret' is an '**independent**' story. It does not follow the Amalgamated formula for Sexton Blake novels —more on the 'independents' in a later introduction.

As is usual for this period, 1932, the story is attributed to G. H. Teed; readers were demanding to know who the author was of the stories.

Included in the ancillary material is the usual advertising for the next weekly issue. A serial also appears: Five Dead Men by SB author Anthony Skene. I have no other details on this serial, which started in issue 1478, perhaps concluding in 1495.

'The Round Table,' an editorial, in this issue is very interesting. It includes two letters to the editor from longtime readers —one of 42 years! A must read for SB collectors.

'From Information Received' column of crime news includes the usual peripheral crime and law tidbits.

Excepting some minor images and advertising, this issue is complete.

This story has never been re-issued. Digitized by Doug Frizzle.

By G.H.Teed — The

A Complete Mystery-Adventure Story of Sexton Blake.

Illustrated by H. Radcliffe Wilson.

A Complete Mystery-Adventure Story of Sexton Blake.

Romantic —being left a picturesque Suffolk manor house, together with a book written by a dead man about the mysterious Secret connected with the same house —but highly inconvenient to be waylaid on the road to it and turned into a tramp. At that point, Sexton Blake took up the case —and the Secret was on the way to being solved.

Before Redpath could make any effective move, the blackjack came smashing down on his head, dropping him in his tracks.

Romantic—being left a picturesque Suffolk manor house, together with a book written by a dead man about the mysterious Secret connected with the same house—but highly inconvenient to be waylaid on the road to it and turned into a tramp. At that point, Sexton Blake took up the case—and the Secret was on the way to being solved.

At **Stillwoods** we are still making progress to make the entire set of G. H. Teed's stories available.

We have had a number of setbacks this year and last. Locally climate change has resulted in fires and floods.

Here are a few books we intend to issue and/or reissue soon:

The Black Abbot of Cheng-tu (19 part serial)
The Hand of Vengeance
The Case of the German Colony
The Latin Quarter Mysteries
Rogues of the Revontazin
The Crime of Stanley Trail
The Affair of the Walnut Desk
The Mystery Man from Manila
The Case of the Missing Athlete
The Emerald Necklace
The Treasure of Bloody Gut
The Crime of the Creek
The Banker's Box
Honolulu Lure
The Silent Woman
Perilous Pearls
The Case of the Scented Orchid
Poisoned Blossoms
The House of Fear
The Clue of the Two Straws
The Mystery of the Tramp Steamer
The Crest of the Flood

Chapter 1.

On the Road to Romford Hall.

WHEN Dick Redpath arrived in England from the West Indies in order to enter into possession of Romford Hall, which he had inherited upon the recent death of his maternal uncle, he anticipated nothing more complicated than the legal formalities necessary to the same.

He hadn't been unduly elated at finding himself heir to an estate of some two thousand acres that paid its way, together with nearly forty thousand pounds in good, sound securities. He was no poor relation. He possessed in his own right an excellent plantation in Jamaica; owned some valuable real estate in the city of Kingston; and had locked away a very substantial sum in stocks and bonds as sound as those that awaited him in England.

Still, he was a perfectly healthy, normal young man of thirty-two, and had no intention of refusing such a pleasant windfall. If he had known that savage struggle, mysterious trickery, and even murder were to bar his way to possession he would not have quailed, for he possessed plenty of courage. But he would have gone far better prepared than on the day he set out from London to motor down to Romford Hall, in Suffolk.

Everything seemed plain sailing enough. After two days with his uncle's solicitor in Bedford Gardens the legal business had at last been completed. The transfer had been duly executed and in his pocket he carried a letter of authority which should establish him on his arrival as the rightful owner.

A tall, dark, athletic man whose skin was burned the colour of light mahogany, he was, yet, by no means handsome. But his face was strong, frank, and full of character, and his manner, though rather reserved, was pleasant and courteous.

He was pleasantly exhilarated as he steered the car through the London traffic and, after passing Ilford, found himself able to accelerate somewhat.

After all, there was something exciting in motoring oneself down into the country to take possession of a place like Romford Hall —a place, incidentally, that he hadn't seen since he was a boy.

Nor did he know very much about his uncle. The old man had surprised him considerably in leaving him the whole estate, and more than sufficient money to keep up a position of importance in the county if he chose.

Dick Redpath remembered him vaguely on the occasion of that boyhood visit and recalled him as a small, spare man with a stern countenance and very bushy eyebrows.

How he had changed with the years he couldn't imagine.

His own mother had died soon after that visit and, almost immediately after coming down from Cambridge, he had gone out to the West Indies.

He only remembered receiving one letter from his uncle, and that was a brief note in reference to some business connected with his mother. And it wasn't as if he was the only surviving relative. There were, he knew, two nephews, of whom he had lost track, and a niece whom he had never seen. Therefore he was still puzzled as to why the old man had left him the whole bag of tricks, though he thought it possible he may have settled cash in his lifetime on the others.

There was one other item that was puzzling him. This was a sealed letter which had been handed to him by the solicitor in London. It had been written by his uncle at the time of the making of the will, and was superscribed:

"To be opened by my nephew and heir, Richard Redpath, after my death."

Dick Redpath experienced a mild sense of excitement as he tore open the flap. But what he found was more puzzling than informative. It ran:

My dear Nephew, —When you read these lines I shall be gone. You will now know that have constituted you sole heir of Romford, with further cash inheritance, which should prove sufficient for your needs should you decide to take up residence there.

This is entirely a matter for your own judgment. I am aware that you are already successful in your own affairs in Jamaica. But it is my wish that you should reside at Romford for a brief time each year if you can make it possible. If not, then perhaps every other year.

I make no conditions or stipulations to this bequest, believing from what I know of your character that you will carry out my wishes. But I do ask you earnestly to arrange to live at Romford immediately after taking possession until you have discovered "The Secret" —a thing which I have been unable to accomplish; and, now that I know myself to be near death, will never achieve.

I have sought "The Secret" all my life. Several times I have believed myself on the verge of making the discovery, but always have come up against a dead end. I can do little to assist you, but what I can do to give you a lead will be found in the small package which will be handed to you with this letter. It is a book which I have written about the matter, and which collates what I have been able to find out.

I do not know what "The Secret" is. I believe it will be found somewhere in the room which I used as a study and library. It has been a secret of Romford for some generations. My father sought it before me; his father was the first to learn of its existence. The papers which he found, vanished during my father's lifetime. More than once lately I have suspected that others have been aware of the existence of this secret, but I am not sure.

Whatever "The Secret" is, it is yours as a part of Romford. Good luck to you in your quest.

Your affectionate uncle,

W. M. PIECEWAYS.

P.S. On second thoughts I shall not entrust the book to Reeve, my solicitor, but will leave it in the safe in my study. Reeve will give you the keys.   W. P.

WHAT his uncle meant by "The Secret" of Romford Dick Redpath hadn't the faintest notion. He had never heard it mentioned by his mother; but, then, she had died while he was still young, and now he told himself that it was possible she never had known anything about it. It might be that the knowledge had been restricted to male members of the family. Or, perhaps, the eldest son.

Did his cousins know anything of this? he asked himself as he slowed down to go through Chelmsford. Certainly, William Pieceways had been the eldest and had inherited Romford Hall. But a younger brother, Amos Pieceways, might have known about it. If so, had he handed that knowledge on to his two sons (and Dick's cousins), Frank and Gerald? And the niece, Nancy Furless —daughter of his mother's sister. Where was she?

He remembered the somewhat vague reference his uncle had made in the letter to others: "More than once lately I have suspected that others have been aware of the existence of The Secret, but I am not sure."

What did he mean by that? What incident, or incidents, had taken place to cause him that suspicion? It was all too vague —it was irritating.

And this so-called "secret." What the dickens could it be? Was it the usual thing that romance went for —hidden treasure? Was it anything as orthodox as that? Or might the person who uncovered that secret merely succeed in turning up some ancient scandal that had far better be allowed to rest in oblivion?

"Well," he muttered half aloud, "the old boy certainly saw to it that I received Romford with all the fixings —mystery and the whole bag of tricks. I expect I shall also find that I have inherited a prize ghost as well."

He was still running through Chelmsford when he decided he would lunch there. He would have been glad of a companion on the journey, but he had been so long away from England that he had lost touch with everyone he used to know. And a casual acquaintance did not appeal to him.

He drove the car —a Chieftain Six which he had bought only two days before —into the yard of the hotel, and engaged a boy to look after it, for in the back was piled what luggage he was taking down to Romford.

On emerging into the yard about three-quarters of an hour later he noticed that the boy he had left in charge of his car was standing beside a large saloon in which were two men, the one at the wheel in the blue serge and peaked cap of a chauffeur; the other, a fat, red-faced man in grey. It was the latter who was speaking with the lad.

Immediately on Redpath's appearance he turned from the boy and spoke to the one at the wheel. The car started at once, sliding out of the yard easily and disappearing from view in the direction of the Colchester road.

Redpath gave no thought to the incident —would have forgotten it entirely were it not for the lad. And this urchin's tongue was evidently loosened by the size of the tip which Redpath tossed him. A bright half-crown was the first coin which Redpath's fingers encountered, and which, in his present genial mood, he decided should be the lad's reward. It was little enough to have such a big effect on coming events; for had he given the lad a shilling or so less, Redpath would have driven away in ignorance of the mysterious

4

shadows that surrounded him.

The boy, round-eyed with amazed pleasure, ran to open the door of the car. Standing there, he turned a puck-like countenance up to his patron.

"Do you know the gentleman what just drove out, sir?"

Redpath paused.

"Whom do you mean, youngster —the fat one?"

"Yessir."

"Never saw him before in my life. Why?"

"Well, sir, he seemed to want to know a lot about you —asked me, he did, if I knew your name, and where you were going. And he had an open eye for your luggage, sir!"

"The deuce he did, my lad. Well, you couldn't tell him my name, for you don't know it. And you couldn't tell him where I am bound."

"Nossir!"

"What did you tell him?"

"I said I didn't know anything about you, sir. He was goin' to ask me somethin' else when you comes out and he drives off."

"Just some nosey parker!" remarked Redpath good-humouredly.

And he thought no more of it. Nevertheless, when he drove through Colchester he saw, drawn up at the side off the road near the bottom of the hill where one turns off to Clacton, a big saloon that looked very similar to the one that had contained the fat man. He glanced at it sideways as he passed, and recognised, at the wheel, the same chauffeur he had noticed back at the inn in Chelmsford. But of the fat man there was no sign.

Still, Dick Redpath gave no more than an idle thought to it. He regarded the fat one as just one of those inquisitive persons who make it a practice to nose into other people's business. He had no reason to suppose that he could have any possible interest in him personally.

It was late afternoon when he reached Ipswich, and, deciding that he could do with a drink before continuing his way, he drove the car into a garage and walked round to the hostelry made famous by Mr. Pickwick.

He had just turned the corner and was about to step into the place when along the narrow street came the same saloon he had seen in the kerb at Colchester. And this time the fat man was again sitting beside the driver.

If they saw him, or had any curiosity about him, they gave no sign. The saloon turned the corner and disappeared, and, with a glance after it, Redpath vanished into the hotel.

Once inside, he decided to have a cup of tea instead of a drink. It was, therefore, nearly half an hour later when he stepped out of the hotel and walked briskly round to the garage, telling himself that if he intended reaching Romford Hall before dark, he had better do no more loitering on the way.

IT was now only a short run to Woodbridge, where he broke his resolution by stopping for the drink which he had refrained from at Ipswich. Then on again through Melton, where he turned off to the right, crossed the railway line, then the high, arched, narrow bridge over the River Deben, passed the golf links, and took the right-hand fork that would lead him over Butley Heath to his destination. This heath stretched for some six miles in every direction. At this time of the year —autumn —the bracken was already dead from the frosts that had nipped it earlier. But the heather was still purple and the young fir-trees that had been recently planted were delightful little plumes of green lying in a sea of brown.

Redpath inhaled deeply. A sudden homesickness swept over him, for, in all these years, he had retained little recollection of the heathland which stretches in a vast path along the coast in that part of Suffolk. But now it filled him with a strong desire to become a part of it, to re-identify himself with it as his people had before him.

Flocks of lapwing rose suddenly on each side. Curlews that had come down from higher ground inland wheeled over the creek, calling mournfully. Flocks of smaller redshank dipped in flashing patches of white as their under parts caught the last of the dying light. Armies of rooks went homing overhead; a solitary great heron flapped his ponderous way from the creek. Gulls sped seawards.

The sinking sun was a burnished disc in a thin fog that rose from the sea, two miles distant. Thin wisps of vapour were creeping across the heath, soon to join up into one of the low mists that would link all the heath with the sea. Yet, just now, it was all poignantly lovely, and Dick Redpath's senses absorbed nothing else. He paid little heed to the sudden appearance of derelict buildings on his right, erections which he had never seen before, for they had been built during the War, and, later, deserted. Now they stood grim and forsaken amidst all the loveliness and the loneliness.

But what he did see just after passing these derelicts was another car drawn up at the side of the road. It bore a curious resemblance to the same saloon which had mildly intrigued him more than once this same day.

And then he saw a man spring into the road and wave his arms. Thinking that the other motorist had had a breakdown, and possessing the usual camaraderie of the road, he slowed down and came to a stop close to the other vehicle.

Now he saw that it was indeed the same saloon which he had seen in Chelmsford, in Colchester, in Ipswich. And for the first time Dick Redpath felt a twinge of doubt about it and the occupants. He remembered what the boy had said at Chelmsford. The fat man had asked questions about him. And here was the same car and same occupants on this lonely heath road.

That same twinge of doubt crystallised into swift action. He eased his foot-brake, eased in his gear lever, and was about to let his clutch in when the man who had been standing in the road leaped to the side window.

And as Dick Redpath's foot froze on the clutch, he found the ugly snout of an automatic pistol pushed against his ribs.

Chapter 2

Lost Identity.

ALTHOUGH Redpath could see the man in chauffeur's livery still standing a few yards along the road, it was not, strangely enough, either he or the fat man who pushed the weapon in through the window. It was a short, thick-set, youngish man with a bullet-shaped head, with hair clipped close, and who spoke in harsh accents that sounded to Redpath like a mixture of Irish and German. In this surmise he was not far wrong.

"Out with that gear!"

There was no disobeying the command with the muzzle of a pistol sticking against one's ribs. Redpath obeyed, sliding the gear lever into neutral.

"Now stick 'em up!"

Again he obeyed, pushing his hands as high above his head as the top of the car would permit.

"Now get out!"

As he spoke the man with the gun turned the handle and swung the door open, though the movement of the hand that controlled the gun as he whipped it out through the window and back against Redpath's ribs was so quick that Redpath hadn't a chance of making any counter-move. Besides, he wasn't armed. He had never expected anything like this on an English country road.

Redpath stumbled into the road and glared at his captor.

"What is the meaning of this?" he snapped. "Is it a hold-up?"

"Shut your gab!" was the snarling reply. "Stand right where you are if you don't want your mug smashed!"

Realising now that there could be no possible chance that the affair was a mere practical joke, and remembering that of recent months he had read quite a lot about gunmen in England, Redpath obeyed the order.

Now he saw the man in chauffeur's livery move towards him. And at the same time he saw a head which he knew to belong to the fat man twist round from inside the other car. He knew now that the quizzing that had been given the boy at the inn in Chelmsford had been no idle pumping.

There had been a definite reason for it. He had been spotted. When? And why? Were these motor bandits such as he had read about, who had marked him down as far back as London, and had followed him to this likely spot?

Followed —no; because they were ahead of him after Ipswich. But they had trailed him from Chelmsford. They knew he was going to pass through Colchester. But they had drawn into the side of the road there just to be sure.

It had been easy enough to follow him to Ipswich, and at that point they had either watched him unobserved or, feeling confident of his intention, had kept ahead.

It was an ideal spot for such a hold-up, here on this lonely heath at the approach of dusk, with nothing but the homing birds as witnesses. But why?

He kept a wary eye on the two who were in the road. The man with the gun seemed to be waiting for the second fellow to do something —something which they both understood must be done, but which Redpath could not guess yet.

He had not long to wait to know.

When the chauffeur fellow was close to him he took a step that brought him to one side. Then, just before he stepped behind him, Redpath was dimly aware of something long and black dropping from his sleeve into his ready hand.

Risking a bullet, Redpath flung round to defend himself. But before he could make any effective move the blackjack came smashing down upon his head with terrific force, dropping him in his tracks.

HOW long a time elapsed from the moment of that terrific blow that pitched him into deep oblivion to his first conscious strivings back to understanding, Dick Redpath was never to know.

His first glimmerings came in the form of conscious pain in his head. Then, as his befogged senses cleared a little more, he was tortured by the inevitable maddening thirst.

He knew that he must take things slowly. He made no attempt to force matters, but lay as he found himself, waiting while consciousness functioned more and more definitely on the waves of agonising pain that swept through his brain.

His first voluntary movement was to ascertain how badly he

might be injured. He could remember clearly enough what had happened up to the moment when he had been struck down from behind. And the swelling on the crown of his head was proof actual of that.

Yet he could find no other marks where he had received violence. Nor was he bound. He found it possible to sit up easily enough, though the movement caused his head to throb with renewed agony. Then he pushed a tentative hand out into the darkness.

His fingers came into contact with boards —rough-hewn timber. Boards were under him as well; and, twisting round, he found more boards behind him.

Getting to his feet, he began to move along, until suddenly a current of refreshing air struck his face. He moved farther, and found a square opening through which he could see the stars. Beyond, within his line of vision, were the dim outlines of buildings. Then he remembered the dilapidated shacks that he had seen on his way across the heath. He must be in one of those.

There was no glass in the opening —not even a window-frame. And he knew that, should the door be locked, he would be able to reach the outside easily enough, for the ground lay close below.

But, finding the door, he was able to push it open. He stepped straight into the open air, on to grass, and leant up against the wall to drink in the tonic night air.

The mist had vanished. Overhead the stars were resplendently bright. A faint breeze was blowing that wafted to his nostrils the sweetness of heather and gorse. Far in the distance he could see the flashing of Orford Ness beacon. Everything was deathly still but for the agitated calling of curlews, disturbed by some incident of the night.

Pulling himself together, he moved across the grass to the road. It was only a few yards from the building, and once he arrived there it was easy enough to locate the spot where he had been held up. If he expected to find his car awaiting him he was disappointed. Up the road, down the road, there was no sign of it. It had vanished with his assailants —with his luggage.

His luggage —his belongings!

The thought caused him to pull up suddenly and make to go through his pockets. But, at the very first essay, he paused in bewilderment. He knew that the pockets he began to search were not those of the suit he had been wearing when attacked. There is something individual about every man's own garments that makes him conscious in a moment whether they be his or those of another. And in a flash Dick Redpath knew that the coat he was wearing was no coat of his.

Nor the waistcoat; nor the trousers. Bewildered in his pain and anger, he investigated more closely. It was too dark to see clearly, but he needed no light to tell him the truth. He was no dandy in his dress, but he did possess a certain fastidiousness that would have rebelled at contact with garments of the sort he was now wearing. They were old; patched, he could feel, in places. And they possessed an odour which repelled him.

He stood and passed his hands all about his person. He knew the texture of the shirt beneath his waistcoat was not the smooth, fine white poplin he had donned that morning in London. There was no collar about his neck; no tie. But a handkerchief of some sort had been tied loosely to act as collar and tie combined. He groped inside the shirt, and recognised the feel of his own vest. They had left him that, at all events, which was something at least to be thankful for.

He extended his investigations to his boots. That morning he had put on a pair of neat brown Oxfords; now he seemed to be wearing a pair of rough, hobnailed boots, one of which had been only half-laced.

Methodically, he went through the pockets, one by one. They were quite empty, two of them being little more than gaping holes. His letters, his private papers, his money, his watch, his keys, knife, and other nicknacks had vanished —every item he had had on his person.

Suddenly his hand flew to his waist. He pressed his body with his fingers and felt the money-belt that he always wore next to his skin and which he had stored with twenty good English sovereigns —rare enough coin in England —which he had got from his bank in Jamaica.

Tearing open coat and waistcoat he pulled up shirt and undervest. Then he ran his fingers along the leather. The coins were safe. In their haste, his assailants had overlooked that item. The presence of the coins was a great relief, but it did not occur to him at the moment that anyone of his present appearance must be looked at askance should he flash such a thing as a gold sovereign.

His realisation of this sort of difficulty that faced him came a few moments later when he saw a bright light approaching. At first he thought it might be a motor-cyclist, so brilliant was the beam it cast. But, as it drew nearer, he knew it belonged to an ordinary pedal-bicycle; and then, as he would have signalled it to stop, the light wavered and he heard the sound of a boot scraping on the road. Next came a curt, uncompromising voice.

"What are you doing here at this hour of the night?"

THE speaker came closer so that the glare of the light passed from his eyes. Then he could make out the uniform of a country constable.

"Why —I —er —" began Redpath, but the constable cut him short.

"On the road and been sleeping in one of those old Army huts, I suppose? Well, you tramps know by now that you can't do that. You'd better get going, or I'll give you a different place to doss."

"But, look here, constable —"

"None of your lip, now, my fellow. Get moving and head west."

Dick Redpath would have protested indignantly were it not that he remembered the ragged and unprepossessing appearance he must present. What use for him to tell what had happened? What use, without a single thing to identify himself, and in those ragged, stinking garments, to protest that he was Richard Redpath, heir to Romford Hall?

The constable would laugh first; then he would run him in. And quite right. Since the advent of motor-car bandits along the country roads in England the lone country constable has to deal certainly and quickly with suspicious-looking characters.

"Come on!" he heard the constable snap impatiently. "I told you to get moving! And just to make sure that you travel out of this district I'll start you on your way."

He began to herd him along, and Dick Redpath shuffled along beside him. He could walk no better than awkwardly, owing to the ill-fitting boots that had been wished on to him.

The constable offered no conversation, and Redpath maintained the same silence except for one question:

"Would you mind telling me what time it is, constable?"

"About half-past four —and time you were miles from here," was the ungracious response.

About a mile along the road the constable drew up. To the right another road cut across that side of the heath. This was apparently the boundary of his area.

"That's your way," he growled, pointing along the road by which Redpath had motored from Melton the evening before. "And see that you follow it. If I catch you on these roads again you're for it!"

He mounted his bicycle then and rode off. Dick Redpath started trudging along again, trying to decide what he should do. He knew, of course, that once he got to London it would be a simple matter enough to receive succour from Reeve, his uncle's solicitor.

But that possibility was not uppermost in his mind just now. He was pondering on the amazing attack that had been made upon him. At first he had accepted that he had simply been the victim of a more than usually bold hold-up. Then, as he dwelt on the fact that his assailants had gone to the trouble of stripping him entirely of his identity, he began to probe more deeply.

"They weren't ordinary motor bandits," he muttered, cursing them in the same breath for having taken all his smoking materials. "They could have knocked me on the head, as they did, and got away with the car, the luggage, and what I had on my person. But why did they strip me? Why did they saddle me with these stinking rags? There is more behind this than just robbery! And why didn't they finish me off entirely while they were at it?"

He marched in silence for another mile, analysing the whole affair from the time of the incident in the inn yard at Chelmsford until he went down under that smashing blow. Step by step, he examined it until he had included every point within his own knowledge.

"They had me marked down," he concluded, breaking into audible speech once more; "had me marked down in London, but maybe weren't quite sure if I intended travelling straight through to-day —I mean yesterday —or not! Hence the pumping of the lad at Chelmsford. And they kept me marked right along through Colchester and Ipswich. By the time I passed through Woodbridge they knew it was a cinch that I would continue on to Romford.

"The only possible hitch then would be if I took the longer way through Eyke and Snape, instead of straight across Butley Heath. Maybe they had another car planted somewhere on the other road. But there could only have been a strong motive behind all this. What was it? Hang it, it looks to me as if it was to strip me of my identity and belongings and to keep me from reaching Romford Hall for a definite period of time. But why? Why should they want that?"

Suddenly he paused in the road and stood as if transfixed, staring up at the Great Bear which wheeled away to the north-west.

"What a dunce I have been. The Secret! What was it the old boy said in his letter: 'More than once lately I have suspected that others have been aware of the existence of The Secret —' Are they in possession of the hall? And do they know something that my uncle never discovered? No matter how completely they stripped me of my identity they must know that I am bound to re-establish it very soon. That means they've got to work fast. If I go to the police —even if I get leave to take the necessary steps at once, and then go to Scotland Yard, there is bound to be delay. And then, what sort of a tale would they think I was slinging if I talked vaguely about some secret. No, by thunder, this is no police job. That bunch has got to be tackled differently. But how? Reeve is no good —too old and, anyway, he would shrink from anything unorthodox. But I'm hanged if I see that gang getting away with this."

He shuffled on in silence then until the first grey of the dawn began to smear the eastern sky. By the time he reached the golf links outside Melton it was broad daylight, and, coming to the bridge, he skirted the end and climbed down the bank to the edge of the river.

Here he washed himself as well as possible. He did not know whether his appearance was improved, but it certainly refreshed him. As for his clothes, he could see now that they were even worse than he had thought in the darkness. Anyone seeing him would be bound to shy off him.

And that worried him, for by now he had made up his mind that he must get to London without delay. But how? He knew perfectly well that the booking clerk at Melton Railway Station would be bound to become suspicious if he presented one of his precious sovereigns. Yet that was all he had. He was, in a way, rich, yet unable to appease his needs. And he was growing very hungry.

In preparation for what he thought he must attempt, he got out one of the gold coins and, clutching it in his hand, started on over the bridge. He had just reached the other side when he heard a heavy vehicle of some sort lumbering along behind him.

He turned to see a milk lorry bearing down upon him, and with a sudden inspiration he began to wave his arms. He did not expect the driver to pull up. He knew how chary any driver would be of pausing at the behest of such a ragged creature as himself. But he took a desperate chance.

"What do you want?"

The driver, a small, ginger-headed fellow with a humorous eye and a cigarette hanging out of one corner of his mouth, eyed the man in the road tolerantly.

"Listen, mate!" said Redpath. "I've got to get to London as soon as possible. I know I look like a tramp, but I've been through some trouble —not with the police!" he added quickly, as he saw the other start to grin. "I've just got to get there, and I can pay for a lift. Will you take me in that direction if you are going?"

"What tricks have you been up to? You look as if you'd been through the mill badly!"

"I know But —look!"

He unclasped his hand and held up the golden coin. At sight of it the lorry-driver's eyes widened, and he drew back.

"Not for me, mate!" he said quickly. "I'm not touching any shiners like that —haven't seen one for years! You'd better not let the cops spot it. That's a friendly tip. No —I can't take you!"

"But listen!" protested Redpath. "It's my own, honestly come by. I've had it a long time, and I wouldn't offer it now, only I must get to London. Be a sport and give me a lift. You can have the whole thing if you will do this, and give me a cigarette!"

The other wavered. But he was a good-natured fellow, and, despite the fact that it was against the law for him to carry a passenger, he yielded.

"Climb in, then!" he growled. "I'm going the whole way to London —to Walthamstow —but I don't promise to carry you that far. I'm not going to get into trouble. Here, take a fag!"

Redpath accepted the invitation with alacrity. He was satisfied to have gained so much, and told himself that, along the way, he would establish his position strongly enough to persuade the other to carry him to the end.

But he did not guess then that this chance ride was to provide the answer to one of his riddles. It was when a certain confidence had been established between them, and he put a question to the driver, that a joking reply gave him the line he needed.

"What would you do? Who would you go to in London if you were in trouble and needed a man who knew the ropes and how to tackle a gang of crooks?" was the question.

And the answer, given with a grin, was:

"Why, that detective bloke, Sexton Blake, mate!"

Chapter 3.

Well Met!

"THE first thing for you to do is to take a bath and get rid of those clothes! I fancy I can fix you up with some things. We are not unlike in size and build."

"That's very good of you, Mr. Blake! I feel as if I were imposing upon you, but I can't refuse. But —you have said nothing about what I have been telling you. You don't think I have been romancing, I hope?"

Sexton Blake smiled as he rose.

"Not at all, Mr. Redpath. That visible lump on the crown of your head is sufficient evidence. I'll think things over while you are changing. Come along!"

The Baker Street detective led the way to his own suite of rooms, and turned on the bath. While Dick Redpath was splashing in the tub, Blake got out a suit of tweeds and other accessories of dress. But he did not throw away the dingy, patched garments in which Redpath had arrived at Baker Street. Instead, he carried them along to the laboratory and tossed them into a corner, murmuring as he did so:

"Tinker can bake them in the electric oven when he comes in."

Then he returned to the consulting-room and sat down at his desk. Drawing a blank pad of memo paper towards him, he began to jot down a few items as he went over in his mind all that Dick Redpath had told him about his astonishing adventures of the previous day.

He had finished, and was just lighting a cigarette when Redpath entered the room, a very different-looking individual from the scarecrow who, despite Mrs. Bardell's disapproval, had insisted on seeing her master.

Blake smiled pleasantly, and waved him to a chair.

"I want to ask you a few questions," he stated, when the other had lit a cigarette.

"I shall be glad to answer anything I can, Mr. Blake."

"I've been running over what you said. I think we shall begin on the hypothesis that these people who attacked you on the road in Suffolk were perfectly aware of your identity —that is, that the attack was upon you personally, and not a stray holdup. If that is so, then it would seem that they must have had you marked down before you left London."

"I told you about the incident at Chelmsford."

"Quite so. But it would go back before that. If there is a strong motive behind it, something more than just to rob you of what valuables you may have had with you, then it may well be that you have been marked ever since landing from the West Indies. In other words, those people knew that you were coming from Jamaica, and were determined that you should be kept away from your inheritance for a certain time at least. And in order to make certain of this they were prepared to go to great lengths."

"Well, they stopped me, at any rate."

"True. We needn't speculate now as to how they might learn you were coming. There are several possible ways. What concerns us is — exactly who are these people, and what motive inspired them? Can you tell me what servants you expected to find on your arrival at Romford Hall?"

"Not altogether. But we could learn that from Mr. Reeve. I do know that there was my uncle's personal servant. There were some other servants, too. I remember that Reeve spoke of a chauffeur and a gardener. I don't know about women servants. But he could tell us."

"I don't think we will trouble him for the present," remarked Blake slowly. "You see, if these people —whoever they are —knew all about your coming to England, and your purpose, then they may have got that information either from someone resident in Romford Hall or from someone in your solicitor's office."

"Do you advise me to go to Scotland Yard, Mr. Blake?"

"That is a matter entirely for your own decision. Actually, though, it is not in the Yard's jurisdiction. You would have to go to the Suffolk County Police."

"But I don't want to go to any police," burst out Redpath. "I want to take a crack at those scoundrels myself. I'm sore about the manhandling they gave me, and I can't get out of my head what I told you about The Secret."

"It is a pity we don't know a little more about what your uncle meant. And now his letter is in the hands of the enemy —if one might use the term. The book, you said, was in the safe at the hall?"

"Yes. But that should be safe."

"Not if the enemy is in possession. By the way, what about the cousins you mentioned —where are they?"

"I don't know exactly. They live in Norfolk. I suppose they are there now. Unless —Good heavens, Mr. Blake! Do you suspect them?"

"You didn't recognise them among your assailants, did you?"

"No. But I wouldn't know them. I haven't seen them since I was a kid."

"Have either of them any profession?"

"Not that I know of. I remember my mother saying that Frank intended going into the Army, but I heard somewhere in later years that he plucked. Gerald was the elder, and I suppose is now the local squire."

"And the girl cousin?"

"Nancy Furless? I don't know anything about her. She was the daughter of my mother's sister, who married a Somerset man. They were not very well off —farming, I think. I've never seen her."

"And your actual assailants —you had never seen them before?"

"Never. The fat man looked like a bookmaker, and a tough one at that. The one in livery was just the usual chauffeur type. The third —I don't know where he bobbed up from; looked more like a German than an Englishman. He was the one who seemed to direct the show. At any rate, it was he who set the chauffeur fellow on to me with the blackjack."

"Well, Mr. Redpath, you have certainly had an unfortunate experience. I agree with you in thinking that it was no ordinary hold-up by casual motor bandits. Had that been so they would have relieved you of your valuables and taken themselves off. They might have stolen the car in order to abandon it some miles away, and that may have happened in any event.

"But stripping you of your clothes, taking all the private papers you had with you, dressing you in the garments of a tramp —there was definite motive behind those things. It does look as if, firstly, they were determined to keep you from reaching Romford Hall yesterday, and, secondly, to strip you of your identity as far as possible in order to complicate matters for you. And it would seem that they went as close to murder as almost made no difference. I know that heath, and I know those abandoned Army huts. A dead man might lie there for some time before his body was discovered, maybe, by a casual tramp."

"What do you advise me to do, Mr. Blake? I have told you how I came to seek your advice. I know hardly a soul in England. I do not want to go to the police. I have a hunch that this affair hinges on that secret of which my uncle wrote. But I can't spring a yarn of that sort to the official police. They'd laugh at me. And, anyway, by the time the police got in action, with all their red-tape questions and all their demands for evidence, that gang would have faded away. What are they up to? Are they at Romford Hall now? What has become of the servants? You see my position, Mr. Blake. Again I ask —what do you advise? Can you help me? And, if so, will you?"

"You seem to feel that you would like to tackle this thing by direct action," remarked Blake, with a smile.

"Exactly that." And Redpath's jaw set grimly.

"I don't know but what you are right. And I don't feel disinclined to lend you a hand."

"You mean that you —"

"That I think we might go down into Suffolk and see what we shall see."

Dick Redpath jumped up and wrung Blake's hand.

"You're a brick, Mr. Blake. You can name your own fee for the job. With you beside me, I feel as if I could tackle anything. When do we start?"

"My assistant, Tinker, will be back soon. I should want him to come along with us. Let us say that we shall have lunch here, and start early this afternoon. I'll figure out details between now and then. You make yourself comfortable."

ALMOST exactly twenty-four hours after Dick Redpath was attacked on Butley Heath three individuals having the appearance of hikers might have been seen striding over the heath road in the neighbourhood of the deserted Army huts, into one of which Redpath had been thrown.

Two of them were tall, almost of a build. The third was younger, short, and sturdy. All three carried haversacks on their backs.

They had not come many miles on foot. Back in a lock-up garage at a hotel in Woodbridge a big grey Rolls had been left. And they had timed their arrival at the abandoned huts to coincide with this hour of the evening, for it was here that they planned to make temporary headquarters.

"Which one was it, Redpath?" asked the one who gripped a pipe between his teeth as the small group of desolate-looking buildings resolved into five distinct units.

"That first one just off the road, Blake."

"Well, I think we shall choose one of the others. The nearer one is a little too easily accessible for casual passers-by. Hallo, what have we here?"

They had just turned a bend of the road where a small clump of firs stood sentinel, almost the only trees in a radius of a mile or more; although, to the left, they could see the dark fringe of woods that stretched into the Romford Hall estate.

What had attracted Blake's notice was a small two-seater car drawn up at the side of the road, and, as they got a little nearer, they saw a girl struggling with a jack lever.

"Looks as if she'd had a puncture," remarked Tinker. "Shall we give her a hand, guv'nor?"

"We'd better. We don't want to enter the hut while she is about, anyway."

They saw the girl look up as they approached. At first she seemed a little apprehensive. But when Blake smiled pleasantly and inquired if they could be of assistance she seemed to regain her composure.

"If you would be so kind. I am afraid I am not very good at running repairs. I think it is a puncture."

Tinker had relieved her of the jack lever while Dick Redpath was unbolting the spare wheel on the off side. Blake stood ready to lend a hand if necessary, but for the moment he stood and smoked, his eye running over the car and its contents.

In the dickey were two suitcases, indicating that the girl might be coming from, or going to make, a visit. On the back of the front seat was a heavy tweed coat that matched the tweed suit she was wearing, and as his gaze went from that to the girl, Blake realised that she was distinctly pretty, and with a shapely but firm jaw. No nonsense about this young woman, was his swift summing-up.

He moved a little closer to the car so as to read two initials that he had noticed on the cover of one of the suitcases. Then he turned to the girl, his smile quite confiding.

"Have you come from the hall, Miss Furless?"

The girl's eyes widened in amazement, while a clatter on the other side of the car told that Dick Redpath had dropped the wrench with which he had been unbolting the spare wheel. Blake saw his head appear, a comical look of surprise on his face.

But Blake gave his attention back to the girl, for he saw the look of apprehension again in her eyes.

"How —who —" she stammered.

"There is nothing to be alarmed about, Miss Furless," Blake interrupted in an easy tone. "I shall be quite frank with you —but you are Miss Furless, aren't you —Miss Nancy Furless?"

"I do not know by what right you question me. I do not know you, and if you will leave me, I shall manage by myself."

"Come here, please, Redpath," was all Blake said.

The young man from Jamaica, his face still registering surprise, came round the bonnet and found the girl's attention had been transferred to him.

"Unless I am greatly mistaken, this young woman is your cousin, Miss Furless, Redpath," he heard Blake saying. "Perhaps you can convince her that we are not footpads. She seems a little nervous just now."

"Are you Nancy —Nancy Furless?"

"Are you Dick Redpath?"

Both of them had spoken together. And Blake moved across to Tinker, who, grinning, had returned to the jack lever after one glance at the tableau.

There was a confusion of conversation between the two whom Blake now knew to be cousins, though how it came that the girl was here in a two-seater car at such an hour in the evening, whither she was bound, and why her air of apprehension, he did not know.

As a matter of fact, his guess as to her identity had not been a very difficult feat of deduction. He remembered that Redpath had mentioned that his girl cousin, Nancy Furless, lived in Somerset. The register plate on the front of the car was, he knew, issued in the Taunton district. The initials on the suitcase— "N. F." —and the nearness to Romford Hall were two more links. Hence his bold but accurate guess.

He and Tinker had bolted on the spare wheel and were casing down the jack when he heard Dick Redpath speaking his name. He straightened up and found the couple standing close to him.

"You were right, Mr. Blake," Redpath was saying. "This is my cousin, Nancy Furless, and you guessed right —she has just come from the hall. She was motoring through to her home in Somerset. She —she has told me one or two things that I think you ought to know."

"I have told Dick that there is a man at the hall who calls himself Dick Redpath," broke in the girl crisply. "He is there with two other cousins, Gerald and Frank Pieceways. I —I ran away this evening after I overheard some talk. Dick has told me something of what has happened to him. And now I'd like to help him."

"Do you mean you are prepared to delay your journey, Miss Furless?"

"Yes, of course."

"But we intend living roughly. In fact, we were about to take up temporary quarters in one of these old huts when we saw you."

"I don't mind that. I've roughed it hiking down in Somerset. And I know there is something wrong about things at the hall. I was going to try to get in touch with Dick to warn him when I got to London. I didn't know then that he had been attacked. I only knew this evening that the man who posed under his name at the hall was an impostor, and that my two other cousins were plotting against Dick.

"I don't know why they do so, but Dick says he can tell me. And he says you are helping him, Mr. Blake. Please let me stand in."

Blake made his decision swiftly.

After all, if the girl had been at the hall (though he didn't yet know what she had been doing there), she might be able to give them some valuable information. Of course, it might be that she had been sent out to intercept Dick if he tried to return, and to act as a decoy, but Blake didn't think so. Her grey eyes were too dead honest for that sort of trickery. But, more to the point, such a meeting —the puncture, the time, the car —would have been too fortuitous for any plot. The plotters could not have known how or when Redpath would be returning.

"Let's get off the road," he said curtly.

"What about the car?"

"Tinker will see to that. Run it across to that far building, my lad. I think you will find it was used as a shelter for Army carts and lorries."

He led the way over the road and on to the grass past the hut into which Redpath had been thrown. He ignored the second likewise, but paused before the third.

"We'll investigate this one and the next," he said, as he mounted the low platform that served as a veranda. "Miss Furless shall choose which she prefers."

He laid his hand on the latch and pushed open the rickety door, and he stepped over the threshold.

He stopped immediately, for lying sprawled face down on the wooden floor was the body of a man.

Blake stopped immediately on the threshold, for
lying sprawled face downwards on the floor
was the body of a man.

Chapter 4

Silenced!

BLAKE backed out at once.

"We'll try the next one. This doesn't seem very desirable inside."

It did not seem to occur to either Dick Redpath or the girl that Blake could not have seen very much detail in the gloom. As a matter of fact they were still too absorbed in the extraordinary discovery of each other for their perceptions to be functioning as acutely as normally.

Nor did Blake give any indication of what he had seen. He told himself that it might be only a tramp lying asleep; though there was something in the attitude of the prone form that suggested that sort of sleep from which there is no waking.

The next hut proved to be an empty barn of a place, though there were signs here and there that it had been used at various times by the fraternity of the road. Still, with the contents of her suitcases, the girl could make herself fairly comfortable —with dry bracken added, and other items which they would cull from the other huts.

"We men will camp in the next one," announced Blake when he had made a tour with his electric torch. "Better give Miss Furless your torch, Redpath, and get something to eat. I'll leave my haversack. You'll find sandwiches and a thermos of tea. Yours and Tinkers contain the same. I'll go and give the lad a hand. After, we'll hear what Miss Furless can tell us."

Before they could offer any counter-suggestion, he was gone. He met Tinker just coming out of the shed into which he had driven the car. In each hand he carried one of the girl's suitcases.

"Take those along to the nearest hut, young 'un," said Blake, "then join me at the next one. Let them think you are returning to see to the car."

Tinker asked no questions. He knew that Blake must have struck something unexpected, and that was enough. Almost by the time Blake was stepping over the threshold of the third hut again the lad was beside him.

But, before advancing into the interior, Blake flashed his torch full on to the form that he had glimpsed only indistinctly before. It was, as he had thought, a man lying sprawled out on his face. And now, under the light, he could see that the fellow was not —or had not been —a tramp.

He noted his garments even as he knelt beside him —corduroy breeches, leather gaiters, heavy labourer's boots, flannel shirt, corduroy waistcoat, red handkerchief about the neck, and a rough dark green coat, with a battered soft hat lying on the floor close to his head. It was the garb of a gamekeeper or under-gamekeeper. His age Blake estimated as being somewhat advanced, between fifty and sixty.

There was no doubt about his being dead. *Rigor mortis* had set in some time before, the limbs were quite stiff. Yet it did not seem to Blake that this was the first attitude of death. There was something artificial about the way in which he sprawled.

Tinker, appalled at the suddenness of the discovery, had mechanically taken the torch from Blake's out-thrust hand, and held it while Blake turned the body over. And, the moment he did so, the cause of death was plain enough. A hole had been blown in his chest from a charge of shot fired obviously at close quarters. It was not the hole that would be caused by a single rifle or pistol bullet; it was the sort that would be torn by the charge in a shotgun cartridge.

"What do you make of it?" whispered Tinker.

Blake eased the body back to the floor, rose, and dusted his knees.

"Let's go along to the next hut, young 'un. I'm afraid Miss Furless will have to know about this."

"But how did he get here, guv'nor?"

"Carried, I should say. There isn't any gun, and it certainly doesn't look like suicide. A gamekeeper, I should say. Possibly poachers, but we can't tell yet. I know there is the usual amount of poaching in these parts, but I have never heard that the locals resorted to violence of this sort. It may be that a gang came from a distance by car —there has been a lot of sheep raiding as well as game raiding all over the country lately. But it means we must do that which we had hoped to avoid."

"What's that?"

"Bring in the police. Come along!"

THEY found the girl and Redpath getting out the sandwiches and talking together in subdued tones. They seemed happy enough, but something in Blake's manner caused them to pause and gaze into his face that was lit up by Redpath's torch.

"Has Miss Furless told you anything about conditions at the hall?" he asked.

"No. We thought it better to wait until you returned. I've been — er —telling her about life in the West Indies."

Blake sat down.

"I think you ought to be out of this, Miss Furless," he said abruptly.

"Why, Mr. Blake?" she asked, in quick protest. "You said I could help. I promise you I won't be a nuisance."

"It isn't that. I have just discovered something that alters things. If you are quite sure you are prepared for nasty developments, then I won't say no. But you must be quite sure."

"I am quite sure, Mr. Blake."

"Very well. I want you, while we eat, to tell us what you can about the situation at Romford Hall. How did you happen to be there at this time? Is it your custom to visit the place often?"

"No. I —well, my Cousin Gerald has been coming down to our home in Somerset quite a lot lately. I hadn't seen him since I was a child, until last year when we met in London. He suggested that I should come to Romford in order to greet Cousin Dick on his arrival. He and Frank were going to be there, and, in the will, there were a few bits of furniture from which Uncle William said we could make a choice. He said it would be better if we did so while Dick was there."

"I see. When did you arrive?"

"Three days ago."

"And had your Cousin Gerald made love to you before you came to Romford?"

They could feel the girl's movement of embarrassment and hear Dick Redpath's half smothered expostulation. But Blake's shrewd mind had gone through the girl's first tentative words. Her answer came after a few moments' silence.

"No."

"But he did at the hall?"

"Y-yes."

"He asked you to marry him?"

"Yes."

"And you refused?"

"Yes."

"You think that talk about choosing the furniture was only a ruse to get you away from Somerset, so that he could have a better chance to push his suit?"

"Not until yesterday."

"Why yesterday?"

"He —he was rather a nuisance."

"Was that the reason of your leaving?"

"I would have left, and that would have been sufficient reason. But I decided to wait until Cousin Dick arrived last evening. When he came —I mean the impostor —I thought it was indeed Cousin Dick. I had never seen him. But he was greeted by Gerald and Frank as their cousin. Then —then, later in the evening, I overheard something that made me uneasy; and this morning I heard one of the gamekeepers say to another servant that Master Dick had grown into a man very different from what he had thought he would be like after seeing him as a boy. It seems that Dick visited the hall some years ago."

"Wait a moment, Miss Furless. Redpath, will you give your cousin a description of the men who attacked you last evening?"

Dick did so; and as soon as he was finished the girl nodded her head.

"The fat man —that is the one who is posing as Cousin Dick."

"I want you to listen to another description, Miss Furless," went on Blake.

Then he gave her a brief sketch of the man who lay dead in the next hut. For a second time, she confirmed that she recognised the description.

"That would be Foss, the game-keeper, Mr. Blake. How did you know?"

"Because either you were not the only one who overheard him express doubt about the impostor, or else he gave his opinion in even stronger terms to someone who carried it higher up. Foss is dead."

The girl and Redpath gasped in horror.

"Dead! You don't mean —"

"I am of the opinion now that he was deliberately murdered," said Blake quietly. "His body is lying in the next hut. That is why I withdrew so quickly when I first opened the door. I was going to ask Miss Furless to look at the man, but that won't be necessary, now. I think we may take it that it is the body of Foss. But don't you see what this all means, Redpath?"

"I don't quite follow, Mr. Blake."

"IT means that a blunder was made in your case. They did not intend to leave you only unconscious last night. They intended to kill you; and they thought they had killed you. That blow must have caused an almost complete suspension of all signs of life. No doubt a test of the pupils of the eyes or a breath test would have revealed that you still lived, but they hadn't time or the thought to make them. But the fact that they stripped you so completely of your identity —left you like a nameless tramp, as they intended you to be found —is proof, to my mind, that they intended to murder you."

"I believe you are right," muttered Redpath.

The girl's hand stole outside the edge of the light from the torch and touched his.

"We cannot avoid reporting to the police what we have found here," went on Blake. "They may make several theories of Foss' death —as I said, poachers, or game-raiders from a distance. I have no doubt he will be well known in the district. Now, will the people at the hall have the nerve to report that he is missing? Or will they just ignore it and wait for someone to find him, and the police to make inquiries? I think that hinges on one thing."

"Which is?" asked Dick.

"Whether, when Foss' body was flung into the hut, they took a look in the other to see if your body still lay there."

"But this is horrible!" broke in the girl. "Surely Gerald and Frank wouldn't stoop to murder!"

"I am stating the position as my experience leads me to see it," was Blake's cold rejoinder. "It is up to you, Redpath. As I said, this thing we have just found must be reported to the police. You can appear with me, state your case, and I will back you up. You will then be able to get an injunction against those who are in possession of the hall. But some days, at least, must elapse before you can eject them, even if they don't fight.

"On the other hand, they may have the nerve to fight. There is only your word that you were attacked by them, and those who actually did it may fade away. As for Foss, there is no proof that we know of to bring his death home to anyone at the hall. There are so many possible theories regarding that, and I suppose he carried a gun. That may be lying on the heath somewhere."

"What is the alternative, Mr. Blake?"

"To report the finding of Foss' body, and no more. Let the police get to work on that. That would enable us still to work on our own regarding your affair."

"Then I choose that. I would give a great deal to take a swipe at that bunch of crooks. And I'm not so sure about Gerald and Frank. They always were a queer pair of tikes, from what I ever heard. I think Nancy will agree that Gerald played the lowdown on her when he got her to the hall."

"Which brings us to the last point —for the moment," put in Blake before the girl could respond. "Just what did you hear that made you uneasy, Miss Furless? Try to give it to us in detail."

She was silent for a few minutes; then:

"Why, I had just come downstairs before dinner last evening, and was going along the hall, when I heard voices in the study. Dick — that is the impostor —had arrived about half an hour before. I had met him, but only had a few words with him. When I came down he was talking with Gerald and Frank in the study. It was Gerald who was speaking, and, as nearly as I can remember, he was saying, 'That part is settled. The book doesn't tell us much that we didn't know. But we'll find it, if we have to tear the whole place to pieces. As for you, you'd better make a transfer of the properly to me without delay, and as soon as we have found the other you can do a fadeaway —back to Jamaica.' Then they all laughed, and I knocked on the door."

"I think we know what 'book' was referred to," said Blake, glancing across to Redpath. "Tell me, Miss Furless, did you hear while you were at the hall any reference to a secret of any sort?"

"Not a word."

"Evidently you were to be kept in ignorance. Well, Redpath, the evening is getting on. I am going to take the car and drive in to Orford to report the finding of Foss' body. By midnight, I expect, we shall have plenty of police around here —the inspector from Woodbridge or Aldeburgh, with a sergeant and some constables. That will make it impossible for us to remain. I shall have to disclose my identity, and explain that Tinker and I were hiking with two friends when we made the discovery. Since neither you nor Miss Furless have seen the body, that disposes of you as witnesses.

"While I am gone you had better get the haversacks repacked and start across the heath. Tinker knows something of the lay of the land, and I will tell him where to halt. It is a spot which I can reach from a saddlepath nearer Butley than this, and I can leave the car at the inn in the village. Shall I leave your suitcases there, Miss Furless?"

"Please. I shan't need them. And I know that part of the estate, Mr. Blake. I can show you a way into the grounds if you wish."

"Ah! I think that will be an advantage if we can permit you to go so far, Miss Furless."

A few minutes later Blake was driving the two-seater along the Butley road to Orford.

Chapter 5.

The Night Prowlers.

BLAKE found the village constable absent.

His wife, a most pleasing woman, informed Blake that he had gone to a village some six miles distant, where, owing to the illness of the constable there, he was taking extra duty.

In a way, Blake was not sorry. He had felt it his duty to report the finding of the gamekeeper's body with the least possible delay. On the other hand, if he were to make close approach to and possibly contact with the hall that night, he would have been handicapped by the nearness of the police. It would be a natural thing for them to begin to scour the heath. Therefore, he was well content to let the thing stand over until the morning.

On his way back to Butley he altered his original intention to leave the car and suitcases at the inn there. On the heath side of the village was the end of the wood that linked up with the estate lands surrounding Romford Hall. There was no fence to act as a barrier, there being few such obstacles anywhere about that heath country.

He had remembered that, through this wood, a bridlepath, wide enough for a car and not too rough, cut right across the road. In the other direction it led, he knew, to the place where he had told the others he would meet them. So, coming to the wood, he slowed down, watching for the opening which would mark the path.

He found it between two giant elms. He came into first gear and bumped through the shallow ditch and into the track. And he stuck to the same gear while he crawled along the grass-grown ruts until he saw another, much less used track on his right.

Here the bushes on each side had gone uncut for some time. Overhead, the saplings almost touched as they reached out towards each other. But, by careful negotiation, it was possible to push the car into this concealment and, apart from disturbing a long-eared owl that swooped, screaming, just over his head, he accomplished the job without incident.

There was, he knew, the possibility of running into some stray gamekeeper or prowling poacher. Nor had he any means of knowing how many game-keepers might be employed on the estate. Redpath didn't know; nor had Nancy Furless been able to tell him. She had known about Foss, and believed there might be one or two more. But Redpath was under the impression that, of recent years, his uncle had taken little trouble about the game on the place.

Advancing from the unconventional car-park on foot, he followed the bridlepath for a matter of a quarter of a mile or so. By this time the wood on his left had given way to open heath. Almost directly in the same direction, and about a mile distant, would be the road that crossed the heath by the abandoned Army sheds. On his right the wood still held, and now he knew he must be getting near the actual boundary of the estate proper; that is to say, where he would come up with Tinker and the others if they had crossed the heath all right.

He walked on another hundred yards or so and, pausing, hooted twice in imitation of an owl. An answering hoot came almost immediately from somewhere ahead —not far, he believed.

Taking a risk of being seen by the wrong people, he lifted his flashlight and flashed it three times, briefly, quickly. Again, ahead, he got a reply, three quick flashes showing in what appeared to be dense wood.

Blake cat-footed along towards the spot, finding that the track began to get more hoof-pitted and rutty. When he judged he must be about opposite where the lights had flashed he paused once more and pressed the switch of his own torch for one fleeting moment.

Hot on this came a flash not two yards from him on his right, and a moment later he was crawling under the lower wire of a ring fence, to find Tinker, Dick Redpath, and the girl lying snuggled together among dead bracken.

They talked in whispers for a little, Blake explaining what had happened at Orford, and Tinker reporting that they had crossed the heath without incident.

"I've cached the haversacks near here," he added. "And Miss Furless says there is a path a few yards away that will take us across the park to the hall."

"No signs of anyone about?"

"Not a whisper, guv'nor. Haven't even seen the lights of any car passing on the road."

"And I met nothing. Well, let's get going."

"What is the exact idea?" came Redpath's whispered query.

"If we can get into the hall and get the drop on that bunch I think we had better face them down to-night. They'll work fast now. Your two cousins will be nervous while there is any risk of Foss' death being brought home to someone at the hall. I figure that they will be working at top speed to discover The Secret —whatever that may be. As for their accomplices, we don't know who they are, or how they got linked up together. But it looks as if the fat one's job is to make a clean getaway as soon as they finish. By the way, Miss Furless, what about your uncle's manservant? What was his attitude to the one who impersonated Redpath?"

"He seemed to accept him. I should, say that he is hand in glove with Gerald and Frank."

"Probably was even during your uncle's lifetime," muttered Blake. "Well, let's go. But, first, what are we going to do with you, Miss Furless? You've seen enough now to realise that there are some pretty desperate men mixed up in this. We don't want you to get hurt. I'm willing for you to stand in to a certain extent, but not if there is any shooting."

"Listen, Mr. Blake. There is a small summer-house which we must pass on the way. It is quite close to the house. I promise you that I will wait there and keep watch on the path. I know how you feel, and I won't be a handicap."

"Good girl! I knew you had sense."

NANCY FURLESS proved within the next few minutes that she had not boasted idly when she said she knew how to find a path that would lead them across the park to the mansion. In the short time she had been at the hall she had wandered about the grounds to good purpose, considering the one they had in view this night.

She found it easily enough, and, at the beginning, Blake allowed her to take the lead. But when they came out into more open parkland —though the ground was covered with bracken here as on the heath —he drew her back and went on ahead.

Quite suddenly the bulk of the mansion and outbuildings loomed up ahead. There was no mist now, and the stars were very bright overhead.

They were upon the summer-house almost before they were aware of its nearness. In fact, it was Nancy who moved ahead swiftly and caught Blake's arm, showing him what looked more like a small heap of ruins than anything else, set among a clump of trees on the left. Indeed, before that night was over Blake was to learn that the place was what was left of an ancient stone chapel.

They stole into its shelter, and, after a swift survey of the interior with his torch, Blake backed out.

"You won't move from here?" he admonished her.

"I promise!"

Blake and Tinker moved on cautiously, joined a moment or two later by Dick, who seemed to have had some last word to say to Nancy. Then, like shadows, they stole across the last fifty yards of park that separated them from the nearest building, the old stables proper, but now partially turned into a garage.

They gained the shadow of the building at the rear. Here Blake indicated to Tinker and Dick that they must wait until he had reconnoitred

Creeping round the corner he kept close to the end wall while he worked his way along towards the front. From here he expected to gain a strategic position from which he could view the rear of the mansion, and, possibly, the eastern side.

He was a little puzzled at the ease with which they had reached so far. It did not seem reasonable to him that men engaged upon a purpose that would lead them to such desperate measures as had been taken within the last thirty hours or so could be so slack as to have no guards on watch. It did not fit in with the extraordinary care that had been taken to trap Dick Redpath and finish him off.

Therefore he was all on the alert for the first sign that all was not as clear sailing as it appeared. And well was it for him that he was, for, as he gained the front corner of the stable, and, pausing there, thrust his head round cautiously, he froze in his tracks. Not a yard away from him, and seated on an upturned box, or some such perch, was a man in the act of lighting a pipe.

Blake did not pause to give him a chance to detect his presence. Round the corner he went, and straight upon the sitting man he leaped. There was a choking gasp as the fellow swallowed a mouthful of smoke, and the clatter of heels on cobbles as he and Blake went down together.

But Blake's hands were at his throat, his knee on his chest, and slowly, remorselessly, he throttled the other into a state of semi-consciousness.

When he felt the fellow cease to struggle he eased his pressure and straightened up. Next he bent over once more, and, getting his arms under his victim's body, heaved him up and across his shoulder. Then he staggered round the corner of the stable and along to where Tinker and Dick were waiting.

He deposited his burden at their feet.

"They're not so unguarded as things appear," he whispered. "If there is one, there will be others. This fellow was slack on the job, that's all. Take a squint at him, Redpath, and see if you recognise him."

He flashed the torch for a moment while Dick bent over the prone form. When he switched off he heard Dick whispering:

"Never saw him before."

"Then he must be one of the regular servants. If your late uncle's manservant is hand-in-glove with the others, then he may have bribed others of the servants. At any rate, we've got this one. What are we going to do with him?"

It was Tinker who found a solution.

"I've got some cord that I brought out of my haversack, guv'nor. What about binding and gagging him? We can push him out of the way then."

Blake acted swiftly on the lad's suggestion. Leaving the other two to carry out this work, he slipped round the corner of the stable once more, and crept along the end wall. But before he had gone half-way to the front corner, he heard a muffled uproar of dogs barking.

And then, faintly but clearly on the still night air, a woman screamed.

Chapter 6.

Underground.

WHEN Blake, Tinker, and Dick Redpath faded away along the path, Nancy seated herself on a stone bench near the ancient Gothic arch that acted as a doorway.

She was quite modern enough to wish for a cigarette, but the urge was not very strong, and, besides, she knew that she must take no such risk now.

Moreover, she had other things to think about. There was, for instance, the strange manner in which she had met her Cousin Dick. She knew now that she had never quite believed the fat man at the hall was this cousin whom she had never seen. Womanlike, illogically, she could not tell why. But there it was.

And she had already discovered that meeting the genuine Dick had brought her a rare pleasure. Perhaps that was because Dick had shown such genuine interest in her; perhaps it was on account of the few words he had waited behind to whisper in her ear when Blake and Tinker started up the path.

At any rate, she was in a mood of content and excited anticipation, despite the danger that surrounded them. She did not minimise the tragedy that had overtaken Foss, nor the near tragedy that Dick had undergone.

She knew now that the hall was a house of evil; and in remembering how recently she had been within its walls, unprotected, she shivered. She began to realise that she had escaped a great danger. The mistrust she had felt all along for Gerald Pieceways had crystallised. She had not told Dick or Blake more than a small part of the importunities she had endured at his hands.

She blamed herself for coming to the hall at his behest. Had her brother not been ailing he, of course, would have come along, too. But it had seemed right enough to come when her own two cousins were there, and it had seemed exciting to be there to greet the new lord of the manor.

She would not own that Gerald had frightened her. Even if she had not overheard what she had the previous evening she would have fled. She had allowed no one to know of her intention until she was actually gone. Then Gerald would find a note telling him of her departure, and he would understand well enough.

Now she was back in the grounds, unknown to him, and in the company of the real Dick Redpath. It seemed incredible, and yet here was the old stone summer-house in proof. She pressed her shoulders back against the old, timeworn stone, and murmured the name aloud:

"Dick."

That Gerald and Frank, with other scoundrels, were playing some deep and desperate game she knew now. What it was she couldn't guess. Sexton Blake had asked her about some secret. She knew nothing of any such thing. But, certainly, since he had put that question to her, she could see meaning in those words she had overheard the evening before, whereas, at the time, they had meant nothing to her.

At this point in her cogitations she came back to the presence of the other three. She listened intently, but heard nothing. She began to feel anxious —to picture all sorts of traps into which they might walk.

The moments dragged like minutes, and the minutes like vast periods of time. Still not a sound, not even the baying of a dog, the sound of a distant motor-horn. Only the brilliant stars wheeled on their implacable way overhead.

She rose silently and stood in the archway, her head turned towards the mansion. But all was as deathly still as ever. She knew there were dogs, and wondered if they would give the alarm. She had spoken to them several times —an ancient collie, a cocker spaniel, and a fox-terrier. She did not fear much that they would attack Blake and his companions, but they could give the alarm, and —

She stiffened into sudden rigidity as a faint sound caught her ear. It did not come from the direction of the house, but seemed to have had its genesis much nearer, somewhere close behind her.

She thought of rats. She had seen field rats running over the stubble, and knew that the old remnants of the ruins might well be a playground for them.

But she had no fear of them. She knew that she need but scuffle her feet and they would decamp, squeaking. It was nerve racking none the less, and when she heard the sound again, a slight scraping noise, she was convinced that it must be rats.

She withdrew cautiously and began to turn, telling herself that she would put them to rout without making enough noise to matter.

She turned fully round. Then it was that her throat underwent an appalling constriction. Something leaped upon her out of the interior darkness.

She emitted one terror-laden scream before powerful fingers closed on her throat.

NO matter how pressing he might think matters were within the mansion, Blake would not have attempted to check either Dick or Tinker as, on the sound of the scream, they turned and raced towards the summer-house whence it was plain it had come.

It could only be Nancy.

He himself waited only long enough to make sure that they had not neglected to secure the prisoner. They had done their work well, for he lay bound and gagged close against the wall of the stable.

Then, pulling out his automatic, Blake sped towards the summer-house. By now the dogs were making a terrific row, though the racket was still muffled, indicating that they had not yet been released.

But Blake was paying little attention to that, or to the shouts of men which arose a moment later. He was uneasy about the girl. He was certain she was not the sort to go into hysterics about a shadow.

And then, while he was still some yards from the summer-house, he heard the crash of a pistol, saw the flash through the Gothic arch. He lengthened his stride, covering the remaining distance to the accompaniment of a sharp fusillade of shots.

He burst into the place, to see it illuminate by Tinker's torch. He could just make out the lad's form behind the glare, a pistol in his other hand. He was pouring lead into what seemed to be a hole in the ground.

Dick Redpath was standing a foot or so away, thrown into strong relief by the light, and, although he had a gun in his hand, he was not shooting. There was a look of intense fear on his face, but Blake knew it was not for himself —it was for Nancy. Of the girl herself there was no sign.

Yet Blake did not need to ask. It was all too obvious. That hole in the floor was nothing more or less than the entrance to a subterranean passage. And that way Nancy had gone.

Even as Blake leaped in over the threshold Tinker stepped forward and plunged into the hole. Blake shouted, but by the time he reached the edge he saw only a short flight of stone steps. Tinker had disappeared.

Something rushed past him and plunged after Tinker. It was Dick, and now, being in darkness, Blake could not see which way he had gone.

But he himself went next, and, finding the bottom of the steps, he turned a sharp corner into a low, narrow passage. Ahead of him was the glow of Tinker's torch, shadowy figures, gigantic blurs against the low ceiling.

He rushed along, shouting to the lad, but when he was still some yards away he and the figures disappeared once more. The sound of fresh shooting came to his ears, and he was forced to slow down, for he came into violent contact with the wall at the bend.

But this, negotiated, brought him once more in sight of the light, and, racing along, he was gaining on those in front when again he was left in utter darkness.

Now he got out his own torch and switched it on. He could see where the passage bent sharply at right angles. Around this corner he picked up several figures ahead in the stabbing spear of light from his torch, and now they seemed to be following a dead straight line of passage for, as he gained, he still kept them in view.

Then suddenly he heard a shout that he recognised as Dick's voice. Followed a bellow from some unknown —the sharp accents of Tinker. Then the crash of pistols.

Blake burst upon a tense scene. Tinker and Dick were standing with their backs to him. Beyond them was a man with a gun in his hand. From the description with which Dick had furnished him Blake knew him for the short, thick-set, youngish man with the close-cropped, bullet-shaped head, and mixture of Irish and German accent, who had held up Dick with the gun.

Behind him, again, was another man whom he took to be the one who acted as chauffeur, and lying across one arm was Nancy Furless, evidently in a state of collapse.

Blake drew up, realising that the situation was one that might be precipitated into murder at any moment. The short man with the gun was talking.

"Back, you fools! One more step and I'll drill you! And if you try to beat me to it the girl gets plugged."

There was no bluff in the threat. The fellow's eyes were hard as marbles as they received the full glare of Tinker's torch. And Blake could see that Tinker and Redpath both realised that he would do as he said.

For the moment Blake seemed out of the picture. No one appeared to be conscious of his presence. The man who held Nancy was edging towards a heavy door, slightly ajar, that was at the top of a short flight of steps. It was plain enough what he intended. And Blake knew he would have to act with absolute precision if he were to break that situation without bringing disaster upon the girl.

He did not hesitate. As Tinker and Dick stood, Blake could see, through the space of about two inches that separated them, the gun hand of the short man. Hand and gun and a part of the wrist were all that came into clear focus.

It was a mark, but deadly perilous to Tinker and Dick if either of them moved. He dared not call a warning. It might bring about just what he must avoid. Nor did he jockey for position.

Deliberately raising his weapon he took steady aim at that inadequate target. Then his automatic spat its message. The hand and gun vanished as if they had never been. Later he knew that his bullet had struck the other on the thumb joint, smashing the thumb and paralysing the whole of the right arm.

But there was no time then to investigate matters. On the shot, on the man's yell, Tinker came into action, shooting once. The bullet caught the man on the steps full in the knee-cap, and, even as he crashed downwards, Dick leaped forward just in time to catch Nancy. At the same instant the heavy door at the top of the steps was banged closed by some hand on the other side.

Chapter 7.

Assault-at-Arms.

BLAKE knew now that any attempt to proceed would be useless.

It was impossible to say yet whether the man who had surprised Nancy in the summer-house was aware of her identity before the event, or had discovered it after.

In any case, if it were now known —which seemed a certainty — then the plotters inside would not be long in putting two and two together. But they could not yet know the exact identity of those with her.

They might realise that Dick Redpath had, after all, not been killed, and that the two had linked up. They might even go so far as to suspect that the girl had enlisted friends in order to make her own attempt to get at the secret of Romford Hall.

But, whatever the theory, one thing was certain. She and those with her were definitely lined up as enemies and as a danger; and, by now, Gerald Pieceways would have dismissed whatever ideas he had had of making love to the girl.

A quick decision must be made as to the next step, and Blake knew it. To attempt to break through that heavy door at the end of the underground passage would be folly. Whatever was going on inside the house could be finished or camouflaged before they could break it down, and, even if they made the attempt, they would have to get axes from the stables.

There was no time for anything like that. Events were moving, and were bound to move, too swiftly. Even as he urged the others back along the passage Blake had decided what must be done.

Once they were through the opening into the summer-house he turned to Dick.

"Your job is here for the present. Look after the girl. I should not have permitted her to come. This leaves us one man short."

He was aware that she was struggling to stand. Then, as she got free, she spoke.

"You are right. I was a handicap. But I shall not hinder you longer. Dick must go with you. I can find my way back as we came, and I promise you I shall go at once."

"But —"

She gave him time for no more. Like a flash she was out of the place and running along the path by which they had come from the heath. Redpath made as if to follow, but Blake checked him.

"She has taken the right course. She knows the way, and will be safe enough. Come on."

He dived under the old Gothic arch and began to run, Redpath and Tinker close at his heels. Now, out in the open, they could hear plenty of sounds ahead, men shouting and the dogs still barking. But the latter sounded less muffled than before. The explanation came a few moments later, when Blake saw the shadowy forms of two animals bounding towards them.

He was prepared to shoot if they attacked, but Tinker passed him with a leap, and it was the lad who proved Nancy's estimate of the beasts correct. Instead of attacking him they halted at sound of his voice, their bounds changed to gambols, and then they were fawning upon the lad as if he were an old friend.

Tinker always had revealed an extraordinary power over dogs, but never more so than at this moment when, even though the animals were not naturally savage, an attack upon strangers might have been expected while they laboured under such excitement.

The paved, enclosed yard between the stables and coach-houses —the latter having been turned into garages —and the house proper, presented a very different sight from when Blake first crept round the corner of the nearest building.

As he drew up at the gate that gave access from the park he could see the brilliant lights of two motor-cars that had evidently just been driven out of their garages in readiness for immediate departure —or flight.

Several men could be seen moving about, and among them he quickly recognised both fellows he had seen in the tunnel, one of them with his right hand muffled in a hastily wound bandage, proof of Blake's marksmanship.

Two other men were running in and out of the open garages, evidently throwing into the cars various objects which it was intended to take away. But, for the most part, the others shifted here and there aimlessly.

This seemed curious until Blake remembered that the seeds of distrust of the present occupants of the hall had already been sown.

They were doing nothing to prevent preparations for departure, but they were doing nothing to help. And this, Blake thought, might prove useful before the affair was over.

Yet he was puzzled. Did the bringing out of the cars mean that the gang had completed their work —that the secret of Romford Hall was theirs? Or were they taking flight because of the sudden, mysterious attack?

There could be no doubt now that both of the Pieceways must realise the game was up. How two men of their standing and position could have indulged in such criminal activities was a puzzle to Blake, although what Nancy Furless had said threw some light on the character of Gerald Pieceways.

But to risk complete ruin as they had, to face exposure and loss of the name and prestige they had borne for so long, could only have been because they had plotted and planned in secret for a long time and because they believed they could commit the crime without discovery. It had been fatal, Blake realised now, to their plans not to make certain that Dick Redpath had been killed and his identity destroyed, as they had undoubtedly believed.

But, whether they had gleaned The Secret or not, Blake was determined that they should not make a getaway. There was a definite proof already against the other pair and, according to Dick, there must be still another member of the gang.

Blake canvassed these different phases during the few precious moments that he stood in the shadow of the gateway. Then he spoke over his shoulder.

"It looks like heavy odds against us, but I'm going ahead! We'll make for those far gates first —must keep them closed at all cost and prevent the cars getting through —no other way out —can't get through here —come on!"

With that he tightened his grip on his gun, and again broke into a run. Tinker and Dick came close behind him, and they were fully half-way across the yard before they were seen. A man made a half-hearted attempt to cut them off, wielding, of all weapons, a pitchfork. But, before he could strike, Blake threw up his automatic.

"Keep off," he snarled, "or if you want to take a hand, join us. This is Mr. Redpath, the rightful owner of the hall, and you'd better join him. There's going to be serious trouble here."

It seemed likely from the manner in which the fellow drew back, that he was one of the servants who had heard the gamekeeper, Foss, declare his suspicion of the man who was posing as Dick Redpath. But he did not join them. Instead, he slunk towards the corner of the stable just as a pistol barked and a bullet zipped into the brick paving at Blake's feet.

Blake fired while still running. He could see the big, bullet-headed man standing in the door of one of the garages, a pistol in his free hand. Blake shot twice, low, and had the satisfaction of witnessing the fat bandit do a back pitch into the garage.

Then he changed course a little, heading for the nearest car. But, even as he did so, he drew up, appalled, as there came a muffled roar from somewhere on his left, and, on the same moment, part of the wall of the mansion was blown clean out, and brickbats, glass, mortar, and burning bits of wood pelted across the yard in a savage hail that sent all but Blake, Tinker, and Redpath ducking for cover.

But the shock of the explosion was scarcely over, and smaller bits of debris were still falling, when Blake once more broke into a run and, as he rounded the corner of the servants' quarters, he caught a glimpse of three men crouching close to the stone steps that led up to the back porch.

The lights from one of the cars was full on them. They were not facing the yard but were hesitating at the foot of the steps as if waiting for the complete cessation of the explosion before attempting to mount.

A comparative silence, all the more weighty for the upheaval that was gone, carried the sound of clattering feet to them. All three flung round as one man, staring at Blake and his companions.

And, in the same moment, Blake knew that he was face to face with the two Pieceways.

PARTICULARLY speaking there was little of resemblance between them and Dick Redpath. Where the one was big of frame and dark, the two Pieceways were smallish men of sandy complexion. Yet there was a general family resemblance, a hint of which he had also seen in the soft contours of Nancy Furless' pretty face. There was, too, a something in their stare that told Blake more than anything else that they were quite capable of the crimes they had been perpetrating, as long as they thought they could carry them out behind a curtain of smug respectability.

Face to face with this menace, they threw down the mask completely. Like snarling rats they crouched at the foot of the steps, while they flung up their guns to shoot.

Blake did not slacken speed. He kept at full trot, shooting as he went, and then, as if the Pieceways realised that here was something far more dangerous than any local interference by police, they turned and stumbled up the steps to the porch, vanishing into the house.

By the time Blake reached the door it was closed and bolted. Nor could he, with the full weight of Tinker and Dick Redpath, force it inwards.

Now, too, the smaller man by the garage had recovered from his panic, and, from the shelter of the darkness of the interior of one of the garages, was shooting with disturbing accuracy. Blake made a final abortive assault on the door, and then turned to Tinker.

"You and Dick drive that fellow out of his hole. We've got to get the other three quick. They've blown out the place to try to uncover The Secret they suspect —will make an effort to get hold of it and break clear. Get that fellow in the garage and bring an axe."

Tinker and Dick needed no more. Turning, they leaped down the steps and raced across the yard, shooting as they went. By now the local servants had vanished, most of them running through the gateway that led to the park. For them the affair was a shocking upheaval that was utterly beyond their comprehension. If the rightful heir to Romford Hall was one of these violent men, they would let him prove it when the killing was over. Which suited Blake well enough.

Using both cars as cover, Tinker and Dick converged on the garage that concealed the man with the gun. He was still using the same cool calculation, husbanding his ammunition, and bullet after bullet whipped close to first one then the other.

But Tinker had played that game before, and when but a dozen yards separated him from the open door of the garage he leaped into plain view, yelling to Redpath as he did so.

Then the pair tore at top speed towards the dark opening, Tinker having inserted a fresh clip in his automatic while he was clinging to the cover of the car.

There was a rapid response from the unseen man in the garage, a hail of bullets swept past Tinker's head. Then, all at once, silence.

The lad crossed the threshold without slackening speed. Now, in the gloom of the interior, he could make out the shadowy figure of a man on the floor. He drew up and knelt down. A low groan rose from the heap, and, feeling about on the floor, Tinker found the weapon, still hot, as it had fallen from his fingers.

But he had no time then to investigate how badly the fellow was wounded. Blake needed an axe, and he must have it quick.

Making back into the yard, he found Redpath just emerging from the second garage.

"That bloke seems done for," was his announcement.

Tinker nodded. He was concerned only in finding an axe. He made for the next door that opened into what had once been a coach-house. And here he came upon what he needed.

The place had been turned into a chauffeur's workshop, and was littered with tools of all sorts. Finding an axe among the scattered implements, Tinker next discovered a heavy spanner which he handed to Dick. Then they tore back across the yard and up the steps to where Blake still stood on guard.

With the axe and the spanner they made short work of the door. But when they did send it crashing inwards it was to be met with a sudden volley of shots from somewhere in the darkness beyond.

They rushed the interior in a body, Blake flashing on his torch to reveal a man squatted at the opening to a corridor that he guessed led towards the main part of the house where the explosion had taken place.

He sprang to his feet as they drew closer, and, after emptying his weapon wildly, turned and ran. But he had gone less than half the length of the passage when a low shot of Tinker's brought him down.

They left him, leaping him one after the other. At the end of the corridor was a closed door. This Blake threw open, disclosing a big square hall illuminated by a flickering light that, at first, was puzzling.

In a moment, however, they saw the explanation. At the end of the hall, on their right, the wall gaped in a great jagged hole. Beyond that was a room, or, rather, what was left of a room. Here it was the explosion had taken place; and here now they could see through the wall beyond into a cavernous blackness that was the outer night.

The flickering light was caused by flames that were creeping along one side of the room, and in this weird illumination two figures could be seen, gnome-like, beating and clawing at a part of the wall that must have been close to what had been the fireplace.

In this same moment they seemed to be aware that their defences had broken down, for they turned savage, desperate eyes upon the three who stood in the hall.

Then, with one accord, they drew automatics and rushed forward, screaming wild invective while they shot in mad desperation.

With his fingertips Blake
traced out the worn and
ancient lettering: "Above
the temple Polaris looks
down upon the folly of
kings."

Chapter 8.

The Folly of Kings.

IT struck Blake at this moment that the two Pieceways must either have a streak of insanity in them, or had become unbalanced through unsatisfied greed.

It was only later he discovered that their mother had ended her days in an asylum for the insane, that their father had brooded for years over the secret of Romford Hall, and that, ever since they were children, the two brothers had planned and plotted as to how they could become possessed of the hall and what it might hide.

All the time that Dick Redpath was carving out an independent career abroad, the other two had stayed at the hall on every possible opportunity, their greed being fed by the urgings of their father, and the casual hints let drop by William Pieceways.

The Secret had become more and more an obsession with them as they grew older, and the death of William Pieceways, the absence of Dick Redpath, and the meeting with an unprincipled Dutch archaeologist, had formed just the combination needed to drive them to extremes.

But Blake knew nothing of all this when he stood against that mad rush. He had only guessed a part. But that was enough with what he could see of their expressions to tell him that they could only be handled as one would handle a mad dog. They were, literally, amok.

He shot deliberately. It was Gerald Pieceways who was the target, though Blake didn't know his name until later. The man pulled up as if an invisible hand had suddenly been laid against him. His arms dropped nerveless to his sides; his weapon fell to the floor. Then, quite slowly, he pitched forward on to his face and began making convulsive efforts to crawl towards the door before a fiercer spasm swept him and he lay still.

It was Tinker who brought down the brother, winging him in the arm and putting a second bullet into his thigh. Then, with one accord, they dashed forward, dragging the two wounded men out into the hall, for it was plain that, unless radical measures were taken soon, the whole place would go up in flames.

And here, Dick Redpath took the initiative. Blake and Tinker found he had vanished, and Tinker was running back to get the axe when he saw Redpath sprinting across the yard.

Blake was hauling smashed furniture away from the creeping flames when the lad returned with the implement and reported what he had seen.

"He'll be after the servants," was Blake's response as he seized the axe and began cutting away the panelling.

They were too pushed then to take note of Redpath's return, but soon man after man appeared, each lugging one or two buckets of water. When a line had been formed, and the buckets began to come along from hand to hand, Blake was able to concentrate a fairly steady attack on the flames, but, for some time, what with smoke and steam, it was impossible to tell whether they were winning or not.

At the end of a strenuous hour, however, it became plain that the burning wood had been drenched to a smoulder, and when another hour had gone, Blake with his tired gang drew back, confident that they had won.

Blake made no attempt to explain matters to the servants. He left that to Dick and Tinker, left it to them to organise a bearer party and carry the wounded men to rooms above. Then Dick telephoned to the doctor at Orford, and while he was awaiting his arrival Blake began a search for what had been in his own mind ever since Dick Redpath had come to him at Baker Street. The brown book in which William Pieceways had written the results of his investigations —his, and a summary of those made by other Pieceways who had gone before.

He found it —in the pocket of the unconscious Gerald Pieceways' jacket. And, taking it back to the library where the explosion had taken place, Blake began to read, oblivious of the gaping hole on the wall, of the shattered and burned panelling on each side of the ruined fireplace, of the stench of steam and burning wood, and the pungent odour of the explosive that had been used.

Tinker, passing, peered in, saw Blake's engrossed attitude, and closed the door on him. And Blake had reason for his absorption, for, from beginning to end of the little volume, there seemed nothing that was not meaningless.

It was plain that William Pieceways had been at considerable pains to collate and classify the results of his forebears' efforts. It appeared, from the first page, that the attempt to solve the mystery had been first seriously tackled by another William Pieceways, grandfather of Dick Redpath's uncle.

His notes consisted of jottings of figures and cabalistic signs, which Blake opined were measurements of sorts. A little later on, when he came to the notes which had been left by his son, John Pieceways, he found that this was so.

But his real interest became awakened when he reached the pages which had been filled by the last William Pieceways. Here was a summary of what preceded his own efforts, with a brief resume of what was known about the business:

It is my intention (Blake read) to solve, if it lies in my power, the secret of Romford Hall. Should I die before accomplishing this purpose, it is my hope that my heir, Richard Redpath, will follow up my efforts, for I feel convinced that solution is one of interest and profit to him who shall achieve it.

Thanks, to the efforts of my late father, little time need be spent upon the notes left by my grandfather. He was able to accomplish little more than to take various sets of measurements before death claimed him.

It is plain, however, that these measurements, one and all, appertain to the library of Romford Hall. My father checked them with care, and I have rechecked them, finding that they do indeed embrace every possible angle of measurement applicable to the room in question.

I do not know the exact grounds for belief which my grandfather held that the secret would be found in the library. I believe, however, that this legend has been passed down through centuries, from father to eldest son or heir of the Pieceways. And, in passing, I wish to state that it was originally my intention to disclose the contents of this book to my two nephews, Gerald and Frank Pieceways, as well as to my heir, Richard Redpath. But I was dissuaded from doing so, owing to certain undesirable inquisitiveness which I observed on their part on the occasion of various visits paid to Romford Hall. I shall say no more on that score.

I must confess that, although I have tested and retested the results of my father's and grandfather's efforts with the most scrupulous care and mathematical exactitude, I have, at the time of writing, met with no real success.

In common with them, I believe the solution of the puzzle is to be found in the library. And it is my belief, further, that it lies somewhere in the vicinity of the old fireplace.

That, as the history of the house shows, belongs to the original erection, which dates from the twelfth century. A secret panel, or some such hidden hiding-place, at once springs to one's mind, and, indeed, if one follows the directions which I append below, one will find an ancient priest-hole, which was erected during the troublous times of the Reformation.

But let me emphasise that this was more than two hundred years after the building of this part of Romford Hall, and must have been built in that long after the first period of construction.

It is possible that, in doing so, those who did the building came upon the secret, and that its real meaning will never now be known. On the other hand, I have been at pains to investigate the history of the Pieceways family from the beginning of their occupancy of Romford Hall, and I have found that one Sir Mortimer Pieceways was the lord of the manor during a great part of that time. He died aged ninety-seven, and in the records there is no hint that he found anything out of the ordinary.

It is possible, of course, that he may have done so. There seems reason to believe that he was something of a hard liver, and held little thought for the rights of others. A hard fighter, a hard drinker, but loyal to his King. But we must not forget that from him there descended the legend of the secret, and I cannot believe that he would play such a scurvy trick on his descendants if he had found the secret and dissipated it if it were found to be a thing of material value.

What is this secret? Is it, as I have asked, of a material form? Is it, perchance, some document which bears on the secret history of the times? Or may it be only a hoax on the part of one of the earliest of the Pieceways?

Whatever it may be, I leave to you this book, my dear nephew, with my blessing, and trust that your young wits will solve where mine have failed. If it be of value it is yours to do with as you think best.

A last word. Look to the fireplace and the wall there, for it is here that I believe the answer will be found. But do not, I pray you, wreck the ancient heritage of the Pieceways. And, above all, take not into your counsel your cousins, Gerald and Frank Pieceways.

That was the gist of what Blake read. There was more, of course —much detail and checkings and recheckings of measurements. But in the prose portion had been incorporated what the late William Pieceways had been able to discover, and, looking at it superficially, there seemed little indeed of a concrete nature to go upon.

But it was plain now to Blake why Gerald and Frank Pieceways had attacked the fireplace side of the room, blowing it into wreckage in a final desperate effort to discover if the secret lay their.

It was vandalism of the worst sort to mutilate that lovely bit of work as it now stood. Ancient as the earliest portion of the house, as William Pieceways had said, it was beautifully fashioned and the top, still intact, had been carved with the arms of the Pieceways family with some lettering underneath, which Blake at first took to be the motto.

His interest was, by now, profound. He would have given a lot to have known William Pieceways in the life and to have had the chance of helping him solve the problem. That sort of thing was right in Blake's line, and, as he drew a chair forward and stood on it to get a better look at the carved writing, he was so engrossed as to forget entirely the drama and tragedy that had taken place there that night.

So ancient were the cut letters, so worn by the long passage of centuries, even though they had not been exposed to the elements, that it was difficult for Blake to make them out. But, gradually, with the aid of a fingertip he traced their meaning, and this is what he deciphered.

"ABOVE THE TEMPLE POLARIS LOOKS DOWN UPON THE FOLLY OF KINGS."

He had just reached this point and was about to get down from the chair when the door opened and Tinker appeared.

"The doctor and the police-constable have come, guv'nor."

And Blake nodded absently, for his mind was already busy probing at that strange sentence.

A STARTLING idea came to Blake while he was engaged with the doctor.

But he could not follow it up at the moment, because, when he had finished with the medico, he had a good deal to explain to the constable, whom one of the fleeing servants had met on the road and brought on the scene. It meant sending for a sergeant and inspector, and it was while waiting for their arrival that Blake got hold of Tinker and Dick Redpath and succeeded in making a way round to the summer-house without interference.

Tinker and Dick watched him in silent and keen curiosity when, as they stepped into the gloom of the little shelter, Blake turned and peered beneath the arch towards the stars that were so bright overhead.

"Above the temple, Polaris looks down upon the folly of kings," they heard him quoting. Then: "Tell me, Redpath, do you remember those words?"

Dick shook his head.

"I don't know them."

"Did you never read the writing that is cut beneath the arms above the big mantelpiece in the library?"

"No. I was very young when I was last here."

"True; I was forgetting. Well, those words are carved there — were cut, I should say, several centuries ago. Listen to them: 'Above the temple, Polaris looks down upon the folly of kings.' Does that suggest anything?"

"Not to me."

"Well, it does to me, and I'll tell you why. Your uncle, like his father and grandfather before him, believed that the secret of Romford Hall was to be found in the library, which is part of the old original building, and was further convinced that it was located somewhere about the great fireplace. I said the secret. My own theory is that they were wrong. It is my belief that the actual secret is not to be found there at all. But I have a theory that the clue to the secret may be there. And I have a hunch that, instead of being concealed behind bricks and mortar and wood panelling, as they thought, it lay visible at all times staring people in the face."

"Good heavens! What do you mean, Mr. Blake?"

"He means those words he quoted," put in Tinker quickly.

"Quite right, my lad. 'Above the temple, Polaris looks down upon the folly of kings.' Those are the words. They do not form a motto. What can they mean? Why were they cut in the frieze of the mantelpiece? What temple is meant? What is the folly of kings upon which Polaris looks down? Polaris is the Pole or North Star. Stand here, you two. Look up. Do you see Polaris? Stand where it appears just beneath the juncture of the Gothic arch? Got it? Well, might those words refer to this place in which we stand? It is all that is left of what was a small private temple centuries ago. Do you see what I am thinking?"

Dick Redpath was pressing forward, peering up at Polaris, that shone bright and serene in the northern heavens.

"You —you mean the secret may be here in this temple, and not in the house at all, Mr. Blake?"

"Your brain is functioning, Dick," chaffed Blake. "Look here — take a line from Polaris through the centre of the arch and mark a place on the floor. Here we are, exactly beneath where we are now standing. And beneath this spot, to-morrow, we shall dig. But, 'folly of kings' —that phrase puzzles me. I wish I knew exactly when those words were carved. The date might tell us something. Before to-morrow I may know. With your permission I am going to see what I can dig out of any old records in the library."

"Go the limit, Mr. Blake. I am entirely in your hands. But what are we to do about my two cousins and those others?"

"That is entirely a matter for the police now," returned Blake curtly. "You have nothing to reproach yourself with. They took illegal possession of your property, tried to murder you and strip you of your identity. They did succeed in killing Foss, poor fellow. Things must now take their course. As for us, we simply overcame armed resistance. Let us go back to the house. I fancy the inspector from Woodbridge is here, for I think I heard a car. He will want to interview us."

AT seven o'clock the following morning, Blake, Tinker, Nancy Furless, and Dick Redpath once more entered the little summer-house, Dick and Tinker carrying a crowbar and spade.

Whatever the result of Blake's reading the night before, he had kept to himself. Nevertheless, hard seasoned though he was, Blake felt a strange thrill as he stood above the stone slab beneath which he had said they would dig.

He had come upon little that would help him, but among the things he had found in his reading were items by which he could link up certain dates and, arriving at one, the possible solution of these words "the folly of kings" had seemed so preposterous, that he had deemed it wise to keep it to himself.

Yet he was almost as impatient as the others to get that slab up and see what might lie beneath. And when Tinker managed to prise the edge of the stone loose with the crowbar, Blake was the first to bend down and seize the edge.

They managed to get it tilted on edge and eased to one side. There was revealed nothing but hard-packed, damp earth offering not a single suggestion of encouragement.

But Tinker set to work again with the crowbar, loosening the pan, while Dick spaded it out through the door. And then, suddenly, so suddenly that Nancy gave a little scream of excitement, the end of the crowbar struck something harder than packed earth. A faint metallic sound followed the contact, and now, working harder than ever, they found that it was indeed metal —seemingly the top of a heavy iron chest.

It was two hours before they were able to dig all round the chest and prise off the ancient rusty padlock that secured it. By this time all four, Blake included, were on tiptoe with excitement, and as the lid came slowly upwards while Tinker and Dick strained at the bar, Blake and Nancy dropped to their knees to gaze upon the amazing sight that met their eyes.

At first it was not easy to discern just what identity the different objects might have been until Blake put his hand in and carefully withdrew one of the larger. Slowly, with infinite care, he carried it to the doorway, and held it so all could see. Then he spoke slowly, portentously.

"Look at this!" they heard him saying. "You are looking upon what it has always been believed that eye of man would never gaze upon again. This —and the other objects —were lost by a king of England more than seven hundred years ago. Go back to the time of King John, that weak, foolish monarch, and Magna Carta. Remember Runnimede and his battles with the barons. Recall when he fled and crossed the Wash, he abandoned the royal sceptre and many of the crown jewels and royal regalia. Here is the royal sceptre. In that chest we shall find what is left of the regalia and many of the crown jewels of the time.

"Who found them? Who recovered them from the silt of the Wash? Was it a Pieceways —one of your ancestors, Dick? There may be something in the chest that will tell us. But this we do know —they were not lost beyond recovery. All these hundreds of years they have lain here safe. That page of history will have to be rewritten. And this treasure is treasure trove, Dick, property of the Crown.

"It must be given back to our own king. But now I think we can understand what was meant by those words, 'the folly of kings.' The folly of poor, weak King John. Before you lies the secret of Romford Hall."

Blake was right. While the whole treasure abandoned by King John was by no means found in the chest —the crown itself, for instance, was missing —they came upon an amazing catalogue of items which, as Blake had said, must be treasure trove of the Crown. Nevertheless, Dick Redpath's share of reward was enough to satisfy any man, and he was only too glad to waive all claim to that in return for one single, massive diamond jewel which, a few months later, he gave to Nancy on the occasion of their wedding.

Blake and Tinker also received smaller jewels, which meant far more to Blake than any monetary reward, for they occupy to-day the place of honour in his collection of souvenirs, varied and valuable, valueless; or merely meaningless, except as relics of the many cases which have formed his career as a detective.

Gerald and Frank Pieceways went for trial on three main charges, receiving each a sentence of fifteen years' penal servitude. The fat Dutch crook died from his wounds; his accomplice, a German, received seven years. The fifth man —the personal servant who had betrayed old William Pieceways, and would have betrayed Dick Redpath —was given five years.

It was never definitely established who killed poor Foss, but the weight of circumstantial evidence seemed to point to the Dutchman as having actually fired the shot.

But to-day there are no signs at Romford Hall of the incidents of that hectic night. The library has been repaired, the old fireplace restored to its original form.

Often Dick Redpath stands beneath the inscription, that has now been cleaned and restored, reading those words that were cut so long ago. And always he turns to Nancy and says:

"I'm hanged if I can understand, my dear, how Sexton Blake saw a clue in that doggerel,"

But Nancy only smiles and shakes her head wisely.

THE END.
[21500 WORDS]

*"I think it's a good piece of work . . . it's better than No. 1 —
Gwyn Evans, on the Second Onion Men Story, out next week.*

From the Red Dragon inn of North Wales' picuresque coastal town of Port Armon, Sexton Blake emerges to join Splash Page in that notorious two-seater, the Red Peril. Splash and he are on their way to pay a surprise visit to the house above the Aberglaslyn Pass, where the night prowler on skis stole the key of the vaults ; where Splash had failed to recognise his old friend the host. It was the man in the shadows who made Blake pause. What was a Breton onion seller doing in this remote part of wild Wales ? It was a question that intrigued him ; that will intrigue you—next week in Gwyn Evans' second story of the Onion Men. For further details, see page 22.

SPLASH PAGE sat up in bed, listening. Through the stillness of the night rang the staccato sound of a revolver shot. Instantly Splash sprang out of bed, dashed on his overcoat over his pyjamas, and wrenched open the bed-room door.

From the hallway below he heard a hoarse shout and the patter of feet on the parquet floor.

"Open the door, Betts, you fool." bellowed the voice of his host.

"What's the trouble, Sir Hugo?" asked Splash, as he ran down the stairs.

"Burglars!" snarled the other. He wrenched back the bolt and a gust of icy air swept the hallway. The door gave out on to the garden and a terrace to the rear of the manor.

"There's someone racing across the lawn, sir!" gasped the butler.

Splash ran to the entrance and was just in time to see a dark figure who seemed to be flying with incredible speed towards the highway. Heedless of the snow, Splash plunged down the terrace steps. His automatic spat flame. As he ran he saw the figure more clearly —a squat, black-clad man in a floppy blouse and wearing a beret. He seemed to skim over the snow like a swallow.

"Stop!" roared Splash, firing another shot. As the figure reached the crest of the hill he saw a short pole in his hand. The fugitive flourished the pole like a wand. And then the journalist blinked in astonishment.

For one split second the man stood on the crest —then vanished.

From

The Mystery of Bluebeard's Key!

For the second time we meet the furtive, mysterious Onion Men from Brittany, and follow Sexton Blake on the trail of the elusive Five Lost Keys of the French Bluebeard.

Here's hoping that you read the first story (in last week's issue); but even if you didn't you're going to enjoy the second, Gwyn Evans has done nothing finer than this series, and —up till now —nothing better than this second story in it, whose background is the mountains and gorges of his native North Wales.

For a real reading-thrill get next week's issue next Thursday; but book it to-day.

From the Red Dragon inn of North Wales' picturesque coastal town of Fort Armon, Sexton Blake emerges to join Splash Page in that notorious two-seater, the Red Peril. Splash and he are on their way to pay a surprise visit to the house above the Aberglaslyn Pass, where the night prowler on skis stole the key of the vaults; where Splash had failed to recognise his old friend the host. It was the man in the shadows who made Blake pause. What was a Breton onion seller doing in this remote part of wild Wales? It was a question that intrigued him; that will intrigue you —next week in Gwyn Evans' second story of the Onion Men. For further details, see page 22.

by Anthony Skene

Now's the Time, Here's the Place, to Begin this First-class Serial of Underworld Mystery and Intrigue.

Now's the Time, Here's the Place, to Begin this First-class Serial of Underworld Mystery and Intrigue.

The Boss.

CURIOSITY can, at times, be dangerous. It was for Max Sutro when he took up the trail of the five men of Harrogate who gathered at the spa from diverse corners of the globe, only to meet their deaths in circumstances both surprising and sinister.

Sutro wanted to know why. The mystery trail brought him to the house of Ralph Olland, whom he knew to be concerned in the affair, where Jessica Hardy held an unusually easy job as Olland's secretary.

Sutro warned Jessica. He thought it possible that the same people who had made attempts on his life might be also anxious to get rid of her. Jessica could not understand all this mystery which Sutro intimated existed around her. She distrusted her employer, though, and welcomed Sutro as an ally.

She did not know that schemes were already afoot to attack her through her brother, Paul. No less a person than Pardoe, the underworld boss, who ruled from his secret den at the back of an

64

East-End cinema, was working to get weak-willed Paul Hardy enmeshed in a frame-up.

Pardoe was also out to put a stop to Sutro's inquisitiveness. His agent, Ha Quong, enticed Sutro to a Soho room, and there tried to dope him. But the trick failed. It was the Chinese who fell senseless to the floor, and Sutro walked unharmed, but alert, down to the car which was waiting outside to take him for a ride.

Sutro determined that that car should take him, instead, to the boss whose brain had directed the trap.

SUTRO opened the door. A large car was drawn up beside the kerb. It was a saloon car.

Sutro walked swiftly to the door, opened it, and entered.

It contained one man, the driver. Sutro pressed the muzzle of his newly acquired automatic against the back of the driver's neck.

"Well," he said cheerfully, "I am the man you were going to take for a ride. You'd better take me."

The driver asked what he was talking about.

Sutro swung the automatic and hit the man across the ear.

"Is that language which you understand?"

"What do y'r think you're doin'?" the man exploded, clapping his left hand to his damaged ear. "What d' y'r mean, molesting me? I don't know y'r!"

"No, but you are going to know me. You will find out that when I tell you to do a thing you have to do it. Do you want another like the last? Or do you believe me?"

The man tried to get a hand to his hip pocket.

Sutro prodded him none too gently in the base of the neck.

"If you get that gun," he said, "I'll blow the back of your head off! The verdict will be self-defence. Now, get on with the driving."

The man asked pathetically where he was to drive to.

"Take me to the boss," said Sutro. "I suppose you've got a boss. Well, take me to him."

The man protested that that was impossible.

"The boss'll kill me," he said, "if I do."

Sutro laughed nastily.

"I shall kill you if you don't. Have it which way you like."

The man appeared to be thinking the proposition over.

"You want me to drive you to the boss?"

"I do."

"And suppose I do it, there's nothing nasty coming to me from you?"

"That's a bet. Now get on with your driving."

The man started his car.

"Don't forget," he said, "that you asked for it. I mean it's your own idea."

Sutro sighed.

"It is entirely my own idea," he agreed.

The car headed towards the river. Somewhere on the farther verge of the Pool, below London Bridge, it stopped outside some gates, on which was painted in faded letters the name of a firm who manufactured or dealt in ropes, tarpaulins, and the like.

The driver tootled his klaxon, and the gates were opened.

Sutro did not see the man who opened them. He was looking straight in front of him. The automatic which he had taken from the gunman was upon his knees. They were crossing a gravelled yard between high buildings.

From there the car ran into a garage with wide-open gates. A man crossed the yard at the double, closed the gates, and dropped a bolt into place.

The car filled the whole of the garage. There were no windows, and the light was barely enough for Sutro to see the head of the driver.

He seized the man's chin in his left hand, and forced the muzzle of the automatic into the back of the man's neck.

"Remember," he said, "you're not in this."

There was a sound of gears. Something made contact with a zip, and the car began to move. It went upward. The garage had masked the entrance to an electric hoist.

Sutro changed the automatic from the right hand to the left, and, with his right hand, took a revolver from the driver's pocket.

"Keep out of things," he warned again.

The lift checked. Nothing else happened.

The two men were now in darkness. Sutro was steadying the driver's head with the barrel of one weapon, and keeping the other in contact with his neck.

After a minute, he said:

"Well, what do we do now?"

"Remember," said the man, "you asked for this."

"That's right," Sutro agreed, "I asked for it, and I am getting it. What do you do now?"

"I usually drive forward. The car pushes the doors open."

"Drive, then," said Sutro.

The man started the car, and it crossed the lift, pushing open the pair of doors which gave access to the huge floor of a warehouse. Around the floor, against the grimy windows were stacks of furniture covered with matting. The smell of the matting was heavy upon the air.

This was not what Sutro had expected. He ordered the driver out of the car and followed him.

The half-dozen men who were working there turned with evident astonishment. All of them were in shirt-sleeves. One or two wore baize aprons. Except that there appeared to be a certain characteristic of toughness about them, and for their being at work at that late hour, the place where they worked might have been an entirely respectable repository.

Sutro asked where the boss was. His guide said they would have to cross the floor, and go up another flight of stairs.

Sutro addressed the men, who had stopped their work, and were watching him interestedly.

"Here, you," he said, "I don't know what to make of you, but I want you where I can see what you are doing. Just step over to that far wall beside the door."

Nobody moved. The driver turned and grinned.

Sutro picked out the leader of the moving-men with unerring instinct. It was a trick of discipline learned in the Expeditionary Force to give orders not to a crowd but to an individual.

Sutro took a few paces towards this man, and pointed to the narrow doorway in the far wall which the driver had indicated.

"Get across the floor and stand beside that doorway."

The man hesitated.

Sutro took another half-dozen rapid paces which brought him within arm's length.

"Sharp!" he snapped. "Jump to it!"

Still the man hesitated.

Sutro pocketed the revolver to leave his right hand free, and brought it across.

The man went down, nearly out, and lay on the floor clutching at his face. The others closed in. One of them threw a hammer, hit Sutro just above the ear. He reeled and almost fell. Someone sprang upon his back. Sutro bent and used the impetus of the man's own leap to hurl him head over heels.

Another man attempted to seize Sutro around the knees. Sutro kicked himself free. Kicked again at the man's face. Until the men had attacked he had been inclined to handle them gently. The innocent appearance of the place that he was in had misled him into half-supposing that these might be ordinary craftsmen. Even now he did not shoot, but contented himself by using the automatic as a club. The weight of the revolver still swung in his right-hand pocket.

One of the gang who could use his hands hit Sutro a terrific blow on the side of the neck. He was not yet fully recovered from the injury caused by the thrown hammer, and this second blow dazed him completely. Nevertheless, he fought with calculating ferocity.

By the time the gang had pinned him to the floor, two of their number were taking the count, and another was cursing an injured wrist.

Panting for breath, and so nearly unconscious as to have no clear memory of where he was, Sutro heard them asking the driver the meaning of his intrusion.

"What could I do?" the driver said, more than once. "He got a gun on me. Wanted to be taken to the boss."

There was laughter at this.

"He's going to be taken to the boss all right."

SEEING that Sutro's eyes were glazed, and that his head rolled sideways, the men who held him to the floor eased their grip.

Sutro kicked and punched himself free, and started the thing all over again. This time the gang methodically coshed him until his insensibility was unfeigned and complete.

He had gone down for the second time, and was lying in a heap upon the floor, when Pardoe came out of the narrow doorway which the driver had indicated, and crossed the floor towards him.

Pardoe was dressed in a lounge suit. The brown velvet jacket and the monkey were both attributes, it seemed, of the rooms behind the picture show.

One man, whom Sutro had punished with his terrific right, was still prone. The others stood in a compact group.

68

Pardoe walked forward unhurriedly. He looked at the man on the floor.

"Sutro, eh? How did he get here?"

Someone said that Stockton had brought him.

Pardoe swung round on the man who had driven the car.

"Stockton, eh?"

His brown eyes were like the eyes of an angry gorilla.

Stockton defended himself.

"No fault of mine. What could I do? He got a gun on me. 'You got a boss,' he says, 'take me to him.'

"Well, I thought that would suit you, boss, so I done it. Nobody saw us come in. Nobody, I can swear to that."

Pardoe smiled, but the smile did not mean anything agreeable.

"But how did he get a gun on you?"

"Why, I was waiting —waiting in Compton Street, like Pudlink told me. They were going to bring him down."

Pardoe lifted a shapely hand.

"Don't raise your voice, I can hear." And then: "Who were?"

"Why, Pudlink and Gissan. This bloke Sutro —or whatever his name is —Ha Quong was going to fix him. Then Gissan and Pudlink were going to take him for a ride. I got to do what they say, ain't I?"

"You have got to do what they say, yes."

"Well, I couldn't help myself. He come down to the car, Sutro did. Got a gun on me."

"Haven't you got a gun?" said Pardoe softly. "Haven't you got eyes? Where are Pudlink and Gissan now?"

"I don't know, boss. They never come down."

"You don't know, eh?"

Pardoe was almost purring.

"You don't know, I suppose, what happened to Ha Quong?"

"No, boss. I never had no chance to find out. This bloke had his gun on me."

"So! He tells you to bring him here and you do it."

"Well, boss, there's no harm in that, is there? You wanted him, and now you've got him."

Pardoe shrugged his shoulders and turned. The gang had instinctively drawn apart from Stockton. Stockton was shaking with fear.

"But, boss —" he jerked out.

Pardoe waved a hand towards Sutro.

"Tie that man up and leave someone with a gun to watch him."

He went back across the floor and up a flight of stone steps to a small room furnished as an office.

Pardoe rang a bell fastened to his desk, and the leader of the gang came up from the warehouse.

"The man you have got downstairs," said Pardoe, "is a nark. He has got to go out. I am going to fix it so that if he is found —*if* he is found —it looks O.K. You've got to tie him very tightly and put him somewhere safe. That's all."

The man who took his orders was a fat man with baggy eyes and a blue jowl. His lips had been split by a punch from Sutro, and there was still a trickle of blood coming from the corner of his mouth.

He said "Right-ho!" to Pardoe's instructions. And then: "How are you going to settle him?"

"You leave that to me," said Pardoe.

"Now," he went on, "I want you to get the boys together and evacuate as much of the stuff from this warehouse as is possible before twelve o'clock to-night. Take the best stuff first. You can run it out to Bow while the daylight lasts, and then take some back to the barges. We shan't be using this depot after tomorrow."

The man looked astonished.

"Not using this place? But I thought —"

"I don't want you to think," said Pardoe nastily. "I am doing the thinking."

Conflagration.

WHEN Sutro recovered his senses he was in darkness. His last memory was of struggling; receiving blows; breathing dust; a light of appalling brightness which snapped out explosively. He recognised this last for the effect of the blow which had made him unconscious.

Despite the darkness he could see the Chinese lanterns. He couldn't get them to keep still. They went round and round. He knew that the lanterns did not really exist, but he objected to them even more on that account.

There was something else. A smell —a smarting of the eyes. He recognised it now. Smoke! Pungent, eye-smarting smoke. Smoke from a fire!

He tried to move. Found that he was tied with many ropes. His arms were lashed to his sides, and his feet tied together.

He drummed his heels on the surface beneath him. It sounded wooden and hollow. He shifted sideways in each direction. Found surfaces very near to him. They, too, seemed to be of wood.

The smell of burning seemed to grow stronger. He began to be afraid. He knew that the King Receiver would have been unlikely to spare him.

To find himself in a wooden box and in a place which smelt of fire suggested terrible possibilities.

He twisted sideways, drawing up his knees. Then, with the breadth of his shoulders upon one side of his narrow prison, and his feet upon the other, he thrust outwards.

The box creaked. Pencils of daylight appeared between boarding.

He thrust again. The operation was painful because he was lying upon his hands. Also, to get the additional thrust he was pressing his injured head against the wood behind him.

He gritted his teeth and strained his muscles to the breaking point.

Suddenly one side of his prison disappeared. He fell heavily outwards and downwards; lay upon his side; became insensible again.

He awoke to hear an intermittent ringing. At first he thought it was subconscious. Then he recognised it for the bell upon a fire-engine. It grew nearer, and stopped. Then another similar bell became audible far away.

He took hold of his faculties and looked around him. He was still in the warehouse, and he was alone. He was lying upon the shattered door of a large cupboard. He could see the shelf upon which he had lain.

He rolled over, supporting himself upon his knees and upon the top of his head. Then he rose into a kneeling position, and by an effort jerked himself upright. He immediately fell down again.

The warehouse was filled with smoke. He could not even see the large doors through which he had travelled in the car.

He tried again to stand. At the third attempt he managed to remain upon his feet. He could hear the distant murmur of a crowd.

The smoke was thickening. Was it possible that his enemies had fired the warehouse and left him to perish in the flames? He was forced to believe that it was.

Hopping along with considerably less freedom than a competitor in a sack race, he tried to get to the windows which he expected would overlook the street

The smoke cleared temporarily and showed him that there was no hope of escape by that means. Outside the windows was an almost unbroken sheet of flame. The last windows were bursting and tinkling down in fragments while he watched.

At the back, the part which looked towards the river, the windows were high. He could not even see out of them.

He remembered the door which led, as they told him, to the room occupied by the boss. He hopped across to that door; and, by banging his shoulder against it, caused it to spring open.

Immediately inside was a flight of steps going upwards. Mounting steps was even more difficult than progress on the flat. He fell once when near the top, bruising himself badly.

On the second attempt he made it. He had hoped that the boss would have provided for himself a second means of escape from the warehouse. There must, he knew, be a staircase somewhere, but it was not there.

He found a room luxuriously furnished as an office, and a smaller room containing a lavatory basin. There was also a further staircase communicating with the trap in the room. That trap, if it were unfastened, promised him the best hope of escape which he had seen so far.

He hopped painfully, step by step, again upwards until he was standing bowed beneath the trap itself. He tried first with his head, and then with the width of his shoulders, to raise the trap. It moved, but it was heavy.

He managed to jump another stair, and raised it further. Then another, taking the risk of a second fall. One more step and he was half out of the trap, the weight of the heavy frame pressing into the small of his back.

He lifted his feet from the stair and, by a fierce struggle which occupied many vital minutes, rolled clear on to a flat roof.

He got to his feet again. All round the roof was a parapet. Lurid smoke was pouring up over the front of the building. He was at the back, at the place nearest the river.

He made his way to the parapet and looked over. Below him there were flames again. But on that side of the warehouse the fire had not made so much headway. Through the smoke he could make out intermittently a fire-float pumping water from two nozzles through the broken windows upon one of the lower floors.

He shouted, but the cracking of burning timbers and the hissing of steam made his shout almost inaudible even to himself.

Near where he stood were two long steel joists. Their near end was anchored to the roof of the warehouse and covered by asphalt. Their far end extended fifteen or twenty feet towards the river, and terminated in a pulley which had been used to raise goods either from the water or from ground level.

He looked at this speculatively. Suppose he were to shuffle out along that boom —assuming that by good luck he reached the end of it —he might jump. Did it overhang the water or the wharf? The smoke was too thick to enable him to be sure. The feat was too much an act of desperation to appeal to him just then.

NEAR where he had come out of the trap there was a lantern-light. He had the idea of breaking the glass of the lantern-light and trying to saw through some of his ropes on its broken edges.

He hobbled over, lay down upon his back, and kicked at the glass with his feet.

It was wired glass. It bulged, but it did not splinter.

After a few minutes he gave up the attempt in despair. When he got back to his feet and looked down through the lantern he saw immediately beneath him the table in the office which he had just left. On the table was a telephone.

He cursed himself for a fool. Why had he not thought of that before?

He went back to the trap, and, lying as near to it as possible, lifted it with his feet so that it fell over backwards, leaving a rectangular opening. Then he struggled through.

There was an iron handrail immediately inside, and he managed to hold this in his teeth until he got a foothold. Going down was more difficult than the ascent had been. He finished at a run, doing three steps at a time, and with imminent risk of spraining an ankle. At the end he reeled across the floor and butted the writing-desk with his head.

He remained kneeling there for several minutes, fighting off the black spectre of unconsciousness. Then he got up, and with the side of his head pushed the telephone instrument off the table so that it fell upon the floor.

He threw himself down between receiver and transmitter in time to hear a man's voice strangely unemotional:

"Number, please?"

"Fire Brigade!" he said.

After a moment another voice came to him:

"Customs Fire Station speaking."

"I am in the burning warehouse near Batavia Wharf. If your people can't get to me I'm going to jump into the river if I can reach it. I cannot swim. Keeping the line open. Call me as soon as you can."

Sutro managed to get his ear at the level of the receiver and waited. He waited for several minutes. Once the man at the other end said, "Shan't be long now, sir." Then, after a long interval, he began to say something else. He had spoken only a few words when the line went dead.

Sutro managed to stand again. He went towards the staircase. He was met by a big cloud of smoke which was coming up through the floor. The staircase itself was alight. The open trap had created a draught. He wondered whether his escape was cut off.

Travelling as fast as he was able he gained the lavatory basin, turned on the tap with his teeth, and held his head beneath it. The water splashed over his head and shoulders. He tried to get his clothes wet, but this was beyond his powers. It did, at any rate, clarify his perceptions. He found his progress to be a little steadier.

As, after a long jump, he landed upon the floor immediately in front of the stairs, his feet went right through.

He rolled sideways, got up, and jumped three or four feet to reach the lower tread. He stood there swaying, certain death awaiting him if he fell backwards. Then, occasionally bending to seize upon the iron handrail with his teeth, he began to climb again.

The smoke was suffocating. His eyes streamed with tears. The trap at the top was even harder to negotiate than it had been before.

He said to himself, with his grim and twisted smile: "This is the end, my boy."

He hopped up on to the girder. The constant jerking had loosened the ropes around his feet, so that he could move them very slightly one at a time. Here, with a fall of perhaps sixty or eighty feet beneath him, he did not risk jumping, but preferred to shuffle along.

The heat was terrible, the smoke utterly opaque. It was barely possible for him to see his feet or the girder upon which he was shuffling outwards. The coughing set up by the swirling smoke caused him to almost lose his balance once or twice.

At the extreme end of it there was a plate bolted to the flanges of the girders. He stood upon this plate for what seemed several minutes looking backwards over his shoulder towards the burning warehouse, if an escape-ladder had appeared he would still have preferred the attempt to shuffle back and regain the roof to the almost certain death which awaited him after he jumped, whether he reached the water or not.

Was it low tide or high tide? He had no idea. If it were low tide he might be jumping into the mud. If it were high tide he would almost certainly drown.

Then came a new danger which took his breath away. A jet of water, looking like a silver rope, came nearer and nearer. It actually touched the iron girder upon which he was standing, then passed on. If it had been a foot higher it would have tripped him, and he would have failed to gain the extra four or five feet of his jump which might mean the difference between living and dying.

Looking again towards the warehouse he saw that it was doomed. So that it would be impossible for help to come to him from that quarter.

He smiled grimly to himself. It seemed that the King Receiver was the victor, after all.

He tilted his body stiffly forwards and fell, turning completely over. The drop seemed curiously relaxing. He wished it could go on and on. And then his back struck something very hard. He thought for a moment that he had hit the wharf, and waited for the pains of dissolution.

Then he was sinking through water, a brown light above him and a taste of mud in his mouth.

He tried to swim, making awkward movements with his bound feet.

He struck surface, obtained a gulp of air, tried to draw a second breath, and swallowed water as he went down.

This time he seemed to be beneath the surface longer than before.

He came up again. There was a boat not far away; a man standing looking towards him. He saw the man dive; then he went down once more.

He came back to life, to find himself racked with pain. Men were moving his arms with rhythmic severity. He was vomiting water.

They said things; he didn't hear their words. Someone gave him brandy. After that he slept.

"WHAT d'you want me for?" Pardoe had sought Waterloo Maud. In his hand he carried a copy of a daily paper issued on the morning after the fire. He opened the paper for the girl to see.

"That," he said, pointing to a paragraph.

The paragraph referred to Sutro's amazing escape. Sutro, if he had been conscious and able to look after his affairs, might have kept that from publication; but Sutro had been sleeping, waking for massage, sleeping again.

"Well, what's that got to do with me?"

Pardoe looked at the girl searchingly.

Waterloo Maud was in a rebellious mood. She was obstructing Pardoe deliberately, pretending not to understand that he needed her assistance. In this she knew exactly the risk that she was taking.

She realised that, for the moment, only because of her hold over Paul Hardy, she was necessary to Pardoe's plans; and that when the Paul Hardy matter was disposed of Pardoe might decide that her usefulness was at an end.

She knew also that people who had ceased to be useful in the estimation of Pardoe were not retired to their estates with an annuity. They merely disappeared! If she had possessed a little more courage or a little less loyalty, she might have gone to the police.

Pardoe was finding her difficult. Nevertheless he estimated with considerable exactness how far she could be exploited. The girl was, for the moment, acquiescent. She was rebellious on one matter only —the matter of Paul Hardy. Otherwise she was tractable, as she had always been.

"This man Sutro," said Pardoe. "he knows too much. I shall have to discredit him. In this you will be useful."

"Ah, I thought that it wasn't for nothing that you sought my company at this time in the morning."

"Naturally," said Pardoe. And then: "What do you think?"

Pardoe looked at the girl with curiosity. Did she suppose that he had any use for her except that she was a pawn in the elaborate game which he was playing?

From some of the frailties of mankind Pardoe was astonishingly immune. He did not touch alcoholic drink, and he was not interested in women, except for the fact that women had their particular uses in criminal intrigue.

He sat down facing the girl, and stared at her with an almost hypnotic earnestness.

"Now, Waterloo Maud."

He went on outlying a plan which his subtle brain had conceived. If it succeeded, it meant death to Sutro, but he did not stress this fact. He thought it better that the pieces should not know too much of the game.

That evening Sutro was sufficiently recovered to make his habitual visit to the Carlton grill room.

As his car slowed up at the spot where he usually parked it, in Lower Regent Street, a girl stepped out from behind another car, already parked; and, walking blindly, as it seemed, blundered in front of his own mudguard.

She was knocked down. Fell rather heavily.

Sutro was out of the car and berating over her in a matter of seconds.

"I say, I'm horribly sorry! Are you badly hurt?"

The girl raised her head, and then let it go back to the road. There was dust on her cheek. Her eyes were wild. She murmured:

"I —I don't think so."

Sutro was joined by chauffeurs from the waiting cars. A policeman came along.

Sutro asked the girl whether she thought that she could stand, and assisted her to do so.

"I feel faint," she said pathetically.

She was a good actress, was Waterloo Maud. Her collision with the wing of the car had been a masterpiece. She had actually been bruised. No wonder that Sutro was deceived.

He asked whether he could drive her anywhere. She appeared grateful for that.

"I was going home," she said, "to Fulham. Going to get a bus."

He said:

"Let me drive you there?"

He was, naturally, upset at being even the innocent cause of the accident, and anxious to make any amends in his power.

He helped her into the car.

"Harpington Mansions," she told him; "just the other side of Hammersmith Bridge." She added that it was very kind of him, adding to herself that he had been amazingly easy.

The King Receiver's decoy knows her job. Sutro is on his way to a second trap. How he fares at the end of the journey makes exciting reading for your next week's issue of "U.J." See you don't miss it!

Write to the Round Table about it! Address: The Editor, "Union Jack" Fleetway House, Farringdon Street, London, E.C.4.

THE ROUND TABLE

Write to the Round Table about it! Address : The Editor, " Union Jack," Fleetway House, Farringdon Street, London, E.C.4.

Your Editor

I HAVE just received a letter which deserves quoting at length. This is it:

Dear Mr. Editor, —In the Round Table this week you speak of old-timers. I wonder if you have time and space for the observations of a real old-timer.

I have been an intermittent reader of UNION JACK *from the very beginning.*

This will, no doubt, make you open your eyes, and possibly you may call for the salt; but you will find I am speaking definite truth; although, as the stories to be mentioned were perhaps published before your time, you will seek confirmation by consulting the ancient archives of your illustrious paper.

The "U.J." is the sole survivor of a goodly company. "Chips," I see, still goes on, but it hardly comes in the same category. There was a trio in those early days — "Pluck," "Marvel," and "Union Jack" — but no one suspected that the latter would display such tenacity and see the first thirty years of the new century.

In comparing the "U.J." then and now, there is a great difference.

Blake invariably worked alone. There was no volatile Tinker; no bowler-hatted Coutts.

Blake invariably got his man . . . the sequel was a foregone conclusion. When once the clue was spotted it inevitably proved the criminals' undoing, despite all their ingenuity of counter-plot, resource, or elusiveness. Frequently it was touch and go with the detective, and his escape owed more to the deficiencies of his opponents than to any particularly bright design of his own. But Blake was always greater than his antagonist.

To-day all this is different. He never works alone, nor does he bag his quarry. No longer is he a giant among men, but a giant among giants, a clever, astute man wrestling with super-criminals.

In the old days characterisation was of the simplest; the progress of adventure leisurely. Although Blake played touch and go with danger, now he actually rubs shoulders with it. Indeed, his adventures have been speeded up to kaleidoscopic variety, vivid contests, and superlative action. And, above all, to intensely dramatic situations. . .

And so on. I'd like to quote the whole of this most interesting letter of Mr. G. D. Wilson, of Easter Road, Leith, but I'm afraid there isn't room. He has skilfully outlined his remarks and recollections of nearly forty years in that letter, and perhaps made up for lost time in not having written at intervals during past years.

However, you can see that two conclusions are to be drawn from his letter: (1) The "U.J." has continued to entertain him year in and year out, and (2) he realises that, though it was good before, it is better now.

Speaking from inside editorial knowledge, I can add (3) to that. It is that it is going to get even better in the future —the near future. (And this isn't just hot air, either. There's a reason!)

The mention of old-timers in this column was, of course, bound to bring letters from others of them, so it's not surprising that the same post contained a second old-timer letter.

Not such an historic one —if Mr. Wilson will permit the word — but still an old-timer. Mr. Edward Sabin has been reading "U.J." for twenty years. He says:

I started to read the "U.J." somewhere about 1912, so you can see why I call myself an old-timer. The "independent" type of story appearing in the "U.J." is not all it might be —such as "The Red

Swordsman," "The Bishop Murder Case," and so on. It is the serial kind of tale that gets over, such as the Confederation series, Roxane, and others.

I agree that the American gangster stories have had their day, though they were certainly a novelty at first. But I think the tales of "Menace over Margate "and "Sexton Blake Saves Blackpool" were about the lowest to which the "U.J." has ever sunk. I almost severed my connection after those tales.

But I suppose there is good and bad in everything, and a bad story often makes a good one better still. So keep on with the Confederation and Roxane series. They are always worth reading at least twice.

Then there is the "diplomatic" type of story, where Blake is called upon by "No. 1, Whitehall" to do some delicate piece of work in some foreign country. Such tales were "The Mystery of the Yellow Beetle" and "The House of the Wooden Lanterns."

In my opinion, this series contained the finest stories that have ever appeared in UNION JACK.

Let Reader Sabin take heart. There will possibly be other stories he does not like —but certainly others he does.

Booked for publication as soon as possible is another Yellow Beetle series. It concerns Sexton Blake and Roxane in Manchuria, in the Japanese-Chinese war. Blake's job is, of course, to combat the schemes of his old enemy Prince Wu Ling, the Manchu chieftain of the Brotherhood of the Yellow Beetle, who hopes to push forward his own plans during the upheaval between the Chinese and the Japs.

The only trouble about this series is that it will have to wait its turn. I have got so many good things on hand that really it's a puzzle to know which to give you first.

Our twenty-year-reader (who likewise finds "U.J." good entertainment year in and year out) will be eager for more Blake-in-the-Far-East; meantime consoling himself with the lesser appeal of "independent" stories —this week's, for instance. Others, less interested in China, will be hugely enjoying Blake against other backgrounds.

Variety and interest, and something extra-good for somebody all the times

But next week I am going to have something to say about an

imminent stunt that's going to be something extra-good for everybody —and for six solid weeks on end!

A WORD IN EDGEWAYS

I should like to commend the anonymous illustrator of "The Red Swordsman," whose drawings of the "Grey Panther" are the best I've yet seen. Another point: The covers used to be printed in a combination of blue and ochre, and occasionally in green and black. The effect was considerably more pleasing than the blue and red that has now been adopted. —*R. C. Dolphin, Wadboroug, Worcester.*

When you asked for readers' favourite authors, it was a dickens of a job for me, as I think there is little to choose between them — they are all so excellent. I have taken a great liking to Rex Hardinge lately; his tales of Africa are real good.

Can't you stage a come-back for Nirvana, Tinker's "sweetheart"? I used to enjoy these stories very much. —*R. R. Postill, The Moors, Worcester.*

How about a breath of the Arctic? It's quite a spell since we journeyed there. If I were to compose a list of backgrounds for our friend Blake, the Arctic would rank an easy first. I'd rather have Blake up against villainy in a lonely setting than, say, the slums of a city. That's one reason why I like Rex Hardinge's stories.

Perhaps you would be interested to know that I bind my "U.J.'s" not consecutively, but according to their class (characters, etc.) and quality. —*D. Smith. Newton Heath. Manchester.*

From Information Received

THIS UNIQUE FEATURE, APPEARING REGULARLY EVERY WEEK, SURVEYS THE REALM OF POLICE AND DETECTIVE WORK IN BRIGHT, SNAPPY ARTICLES BOTH GRAVE AND GAY.

SELF-ACCUSED!

NOT the least amazing feature of many big crime cases, where the police are busy on the hue and cry after some unknown crook, is the number of people who come forward voluntarily to the police and willfully, but without any justification implicate themselves in the crime.

Sometimes they definitely accuse themselves of being guilty, laying before the police elaborate confessions, and the police, after a painstaking inquiry into their statements, have to send them on their way with a caution not to involve themselves in crime at grave risk to themselves, and at serious hindrance to the law.

A perverted sense of self-importance, no matter how harsh or unfavourably the limelight of publicity may shine on them, is usually the motive behind such misguided "penitence." Overlooking the horror of a crime, these self-accusers see merely the chance of getting their names into the paper, and of being talked about. But few have gone to the lengths of a young German, Otto Weiss of Breslau. He went to the police and informed them that he had defrauded a firm of some money. As young Weiss had previously been imprisoned for minor crimes, credence was given to his story, and he was placed in the cells, pending inquiries.

Then it came to light that not only was Weiss innocent, but the crime itself was an invention!

There was a bigger surprise when Weiss, told that he might go free, begged to be allowed to stay in his cell. The regular hours, the certainty of meals, the lack of responsibility, and the restful repose had, he claimed, become a physical necessity for him.

THE LAW'S FLAWS.

For those who want to break the law, the safety-first rule seems to be: follow the letter, dodge the spirit.

"THERE was never a law made yet that you couldn't drive a coach-and-four through." So runs saying; which is merely another way of suggesting, in modern language, that it is possible to wangle a way round any law if one has a mind to.

When the laws of the land are hammered into shape at Westminster, Parliament naturally tries to foresee any loopholes, and to design the wording of the Act to prevent any evasion. But with so many equally ingenious minds at work outside, it's often a case of "where there's a will there's a way."

Means have been found to get round practically every law, but particularly those involving taxation or restrictions which people find irksome.

When the Entertainment Tax first came in —a very unpopular measure —it was announced that theatrical shows would be taxed. Cabarets in hotels were not, however. By way of protesting at this, a London theatre devised a scheme to sell their patrons boxes of chocolates instead of tickets. These would admit the theatregoers to various parts of the house, the price, of course, being adjusted to cover both the chocolates and the seat.

In this way, it was intended, no revenue would be payable because no tickets had been sold.

But this stunt was promptly nipped in the bud.

THEN there is Income Tax —a difficult enough proposition to get around; yet it has been done.

Big landowners discovered that the ownership of their estates was ruining them. Although these estates were supposed in theory to bring in a certain income, in practice they did not, but the tax had to be paid just the same.

Or rather, it does if the land is owned by a private individual. If it is owned by a limited company, however, only the dividends are taxable.

The landowners' retort to the Income Tax man's demand was to turn themselves into limited companies, so that now there are dozens of peers of the realm, and others, who can write "Ltd." after their names, as well as letters signifying the more usual honours and decorations. By so doing they save themselves, in some cases, thousands of pounds every year.

It is only fair, however, to point out that this money saved is not money earned, and that unless they were able to dodge the letter of the law in this way they would speedily become bankrupt.

Much less excusable was the cute idea put forward by a French firm a few weeks ago to try and defeat the Customs duty on ladies' dresses imported into this country.

The duties are based on the value of the articles concerned, and paid by the exporter —in this case the Paris firm of dressmakers. The British buyer, of course, pays more accordingly.

To obtain their trade, the French exporters offered the bait of a lower price if the British buyer would co-operate in their tax-dodging scheme, which was simply (but ingeniously) this: The French firm proposed to supply two invoices for each purchase; one invoice represented the cost of the materials and labour, which was taxable, the other was the fee for the designer's skill and artistry in evolving the dress.

There is, of course, no tax payable on mere brain-waves, and as this would amount to at least half of the price charged, the Revenue would lose fifty per cent of its dues.

There is a risk in dodging the law in this way, though. Importers are required to make a declaration of the full cost of the articles they bring into the country, and if they fail to do so there is a method of reminding them which they find very costly.

AN instance of the foreigner "getting away with it occurred, on the other hand, when 50,000 pairs of silk stockings were landed in London from abroad.

The Customs authorities charged the duty payable, but estimated that the country had lost about £10.000 on the deal. They would have received that amount more than they did, had the articles been taxed as *stockings*. All they could do was to impose the duty on silk tissue, and charge by weight.

Yet they were stockings, except in the strict letter of the law. *The seams had merely been left unsewn.* The shapes had been woven and cut in such a way as to make it a quick and inexpensive process to sew the seams —and John Bull lost thousands of pounds through a flaw in the law.

This summer the "Come to Britain" campaign will prevent our seaside resorts being hampered by gloomy restrictions, but last season the town council of a certain coast town banned bands in the streets on the ground of "noise."

The section of the townsfolk who did not agree had no difficulty in getting past that one. They merely arranged with various boarding-house keepers to allow the band to play in their front gardens, which, not being public places, were outside official control; and all the music-hating councillors and residents could do was to mutter indignantly among themselves.

But if the spirit of the law can be evaded by following it in the letter, so in the same way can it sometimes be made to function where its designers did not intend. One case was when a golf course at Oxford was so laid out that players had to drive across a public footpath. Appealing to the Ministry of Health, the local council were told that there was no law to prevent it.

They retorted that there was —the Firearms' Act, which forbids the propelling of any missile across the highway.

"And isn't a golf ball a missile?" asked the council.

An old wall vanished from round this privileged window; a new wall will arise—and the legal light be uninterrupted. Thus may the law be satisfied.

Then there is the matter of the law about Ancient Lights, causing the curious building effect shown in our picture of a building which is being demolished at Nottingham.

The owner of a window which has had uninterrupted light for

twenty years can claim the right of forbidding the erection of another building adjacent which would shut out the light; and in this case, when it became necessary to pull down the old house containing the "ancient light," the owner apparently decided to rely on the letter of the law to allow him to keep his privilege.

The actual window was left in position in the air, supported on scaffold poles, while the walls all round it were removed; so that he can justly claim in case of need that the window has had its uninterrupted light and, therefore, retains its legal privilege.

DUMB Prisoners DIED
if they refused to speak in their defence. Literally, the judge brought pressure to bear.

"UP to time of going to press the prisoner has refused to give evidence. An early statement is expected, however." So might the jocular journalist of an earlier age have both accurately reported the facts and punned on the punishment.

To explain: in former times it was the custom, when a prisoner remained mute and would not plead either Guilty or Not Guilty, to place him under heavy weights until he consented to do so —or else until he died.

Luckily those times and that custom are long past, or we should now be having the unimaginable horror of seeing that penalty inflicted on a young girl of twenty-one.

At the Juvenile Court of the Guildhall, London, was a girl who appeared to be no older than sixteen. She had been found wandering. Confronted with the magistrate, she turned her back and refused to speak. No coaxing or appeals could move her from her muteness. Baffled, the magistrate put her back for inquiries to be made.

She came before him a week later, and again remained dumb. A witness, however, was present to say that the girl was known. She was Clara Eileen Shaw —or that was the name she had given on the previous occasion —and was older than her apparent age, being actually about twenty-one.

Even when this evidence was given, and when the witness alleged that the girl had a police history, little Clara Shaw persisted in her perversity. In legal language, she refused to plead.

A somewhat difficult case to deal with under modern conditions;

though usually, when a prisoner in a criminal case will not say whether he is Guilty or Not Guilty, the judge orders a plea of Not Guilty to be entered, and the trial goes ahead.

Between that mere formality and the barbarous punishment of pressing to death are several centuries of humanitarian progress. The last memento of it lingered till the year 1904, when Newgate Prison was demolished to make way for London's new Central Criminal Court, the Old Bailey. A large, stone-paved yard between the high walls of two blocks of the old Newgate cell-blocks was known as the Press Yard —a terribly sinister name when one realises what it meant, and that it had nothing to do with journalism, as many may have supposed.

It was on that same spot, but in the earlier Press Yard, which was part of the prison that previously stood on the site of Newgate, that in 1741 one of the last authentic instances of pressing to death occurred; for even by the far from squeamish standards of the eighteenth century it was rather too savage to be allowed to continue.

Newgate's Press Yard, on the site of the earlier one of the ancient Old Bailey.

IT was not a common punishment by any means, but there are several cases of it mentioned by historians of the period. In 1651 four men accused of robbery refused to speak, and as they persisted in their contempt of court, were pressed to death.

There appear to have been various ways of doing this, for accounts vary. The details include tying ropes to the prisoner's limbs and stretching them in different directions as he lay on his back, and then piling weights of iron or stone on him. In other instances mention is made of a sort of rack or framework on which the weights were supported, the framework resting on the prisoner's body.

Eight years later, in 1659, a Major Strangeways was accused of murder, refused to plead, and was likewise pressed to death.

Terse Tales.
HABIT.
IN Vienna a labourer was asked by the judge to justify his action in throwing his wife out of a fourth-floor window. Said the labourer:
"We had just moved in, your honour."
"What has that to do with it?"
"In our last house we lived on the ground floor." explained the prisoner.

ISSUE.
AT Southend Police Court a wife testified that she and her husband had eighteen children.
Said the father: "I make it only twelve."
The wife was emphatic about the correctness of her count; the husband about the correctness of his. Each failed to convince the other.

PAINTER.
IN the Rue Caulaincour, Paris, a house painter entered a bus carrying an open can of white paint.
Objecting to the smell, the risk of splashes, the conductor and passengers remonstrated.
"Ah, you don't like paint?" exclaimed the man; and with the brush showered white —bus, passengers, and conductor. Pushed into the street, the painter was manhandled by his victims.
The police rescued him. He recovered from his injuries in a prison hospital bed, prior to being charged with assault by splashing.

• •   •   •   •

It is likely that he and others like him may have been impelled to their stubborn silence by a sort of unselfish heroism. Many of the old crimes carried, as part of the penalty, the confiscation of the criminal's possessions; but where there was no plea and no trial the prisoner's dependents were not robbed of his estate. Therefore, when a man refused to plead, he might have decided on the terrible alternative of pressing to death in order to save his family from want.

In earlier centuries the punishment was designed frankly as a torture. As variations on the custom there were the punishments of putting a mute prisoner into a dark underground cell, where he was laid on the floor naked and placed under as great a weight as he could bear, and fed on scraps of bread and sips of water till he died, or till he answered.

A highwayman named Spiggott died in the Press Yard of the Old Bailey about the year 1720, and twenty years elapsed before the next, and final one. This again was a highway robber, one Henry Cook.

The chronicle of the time stated that the mute prisoners were not then allowed to undergo such a length of torture, but had so great a weight put upon them that they soon expired.

So that, even in 1741, savagery masquerading as criminal punishment was beginning to die out, and the idea of torture beginning to give way to things a little more humane.

You can cut out the Competition pictures without mutilating the Sexton Blake story.

This is done so that you can hand on this copy of **"U.J."** *to a friend when you are finished with it. He will appreciate this fine yarn, too.*

WIN THE GREATEST PICTURE PRIZE IN

Our "Grand National!"

£20 A WEEK FOR LIFE OR £5,000 CASH DOWN

MUST BE WON

NO CLAIMS *Every entry will be fully Checked.*

Colossal Competition

Second Prize £200. Third Prize £50.

ONLY FOUR MORE SETS TO COME!

FORTUNES will be won and lost over the Grand National in a week or two's time. But don't forget that a magnificent fortune awaits the winner of *our* "Grand National"! The great race for this prize has already begun—in fact, there are only four more weeks to go now. But you can quite easily join in the running now for £5,000 "Cash Down," or £20 a Week for Life, by asking your newsagent for the four previous issues of "Union Jack" (dated February 13th, 20th, and March 5th, respectively), which between them contain all the previous puzzle-sets. Some-one *must* win that gigantic prize, remember —it may be you.

How You Can Win! All you have to do is to solve ten sets of simple puzzle-pictures. Soon the Grand National race itself will be run, and therefore we are representing in these puzzles the names of National winners and runners and other well-known steeplechasers.

The first five sets of puzzles have already appeared, and here you have the Sixth Set of them to solve. They are all quite straight-forward, and to help you still further we have already given the list from which all the horses' names in the competition have been taken. So really it is just a matter of fitting the right name to each picture to win that huge Life-Income or £5,000!

In the space under each picture write IN INK and in capital letters, the name you think it denotes. Then cut out this set and keep it with the others until next week, when we shall give you six more of these puzzles to solve—and so on, for only four more weeks.

With the tenth and final set we shall tell you how and where to send in your entries. No claims will be asked for in this com-petition, as every entry received will be fully examined. The only charge in connection with the contest is the small one of 3d., to be paid *in stamps* at the end of the contest, as a checking and registration fee. The com-petition rules were printed earlier in the contest, and will be given again later.

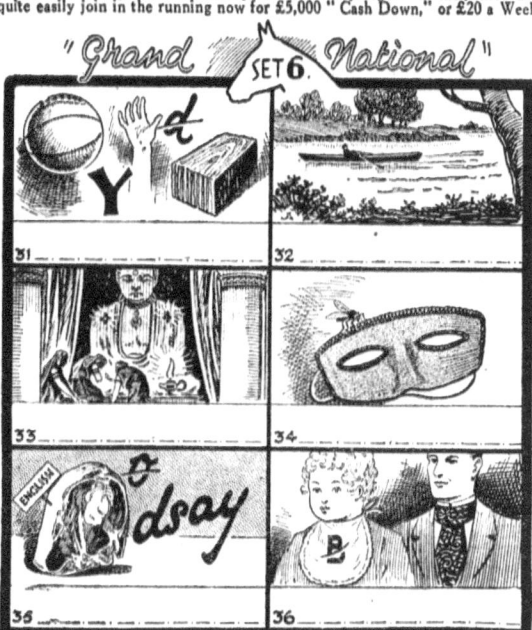

"Grand **SET 6** National"

31 ___ 32 ___

33 ___ 34 ___

35 ___ 36 ___

DON'T SEND IN ANY SETS YET—KEEP THEM UNTIL THE FINAL WEEK.

Contest

FORTUNES will be won and lost over the Grand National in a week or two's time. But don't forget that a magnificent fortune awaits the winner of *our* "Grand National"! The great race for this prize has already begun —in fact, there are only four more weeks to go now. But you can quite easily join in the running now for £5,000 "Cash Down," or £20 a Week for Life, by asking your newsagent for the four previous issues of "Union Jack" (dated February 13th, 20th, and 27th, and March 5th, respectively), which between them contain all the previous puzzle-sets. Someone *must* win that gigantic prize, remember —it may be you.

How You Can Win! All you have to do is to solve ten sets of simple puzzle-pictures.

Soon the Grand National race itself will be run, and therefore we are representing in these puzzles the names of National winners and runners and other well-known steeplechasers.

The first five sets of puzzles have already appeared, and here you have the Sixth Set of them to solve. They are all quite straightforward, and to help you still further we have already given the list from which all the horses' names in the competition have been taken. So really it is just a matter of fitting the right name to each picture to win that huge Life-Income or £5,000!

In the space under each picture write IN INK and in capital letters, the name you think it denotes. Then cut out this set and keep it with the others until next week, when we shall give you six more of these puzzles to solve —and so on, for only four more weeks.

With the tenth and final set we shall tell you how and where to send in your entries.

No claims will be asked for in this competition, as every entry received will be fully examined. The only charge in connection with the contest is the small one of 3d., to be paid *in stamps* at the end of the contest, as a checking and registration fee. The competition rules were printed earlier in the contest, and will be given again later.

DON'T SEND IN ANY SETS YET —KEEP THEM UNTIL THE FINAL WEEK